Stories of King Arthur and His Knights

Retold from Malory's Morte d'Arthur

"We have from the kind Creator a variety of mental powers, to which we must not neglect giving their proper culture in our earliest years, and which cannot be cultivated either by logic or metaphysics, Latin or Greek. We have an imagination, before which, since it should not seize upon the very first conceptions that chance to present themselves, we ought to place the fittest and most beautiful images, and thus accustom and practise the mind to recognise and love the beautiful everywhere."

Quoted from Wieland by Goethe in his Autobiography

Start Publishing PD LLC

Manufactured in the United States of America

Cover art: Shutterstock/Taisiya Kozorez

Cover design: Jennifer Do

10 9 8 7 6 5 4 3 2 1

ISBN 979-8-8809-1209-4

Stories of King Arthur and His Knights

Retold from Malory's Morte d'Arthur

by U. Waldo Cutler

Table of Contents

Introduction

Among the best liked stories of five or six hundred years ago were those which told of chivalrous deeds—of joust and tourney and knightly adventure. To be sure, these stories were not set forth in printed books, for there were no printed books as early as the times of the first three King Edwards, and few people could have read them if there had been any. But children and grown people alike were eager to hear these old-time tales read or recited by the minstrels, and the interest in them has continued in some measure through all the changing years and tastes. We now, in the times of the seventh King Edward, still find them far more worth our while than many modern stories. For us they have a special interest, because of home setting and Christian basis, and they may well share in our attention with the legends of Greece and Rome.

In these early romances of chivalry, Arthur and his knights of the Round Table are by far the most popular heroes, and the finding of the Holy Grail is the highest achievement of knightly valour. The material for the Arthur stories came from many countries and from many different periods of history. Much of it is wholly fanciful, but the writers connected all the incidents directly or indirectly with the old Briton king of the fifth century, who was the model of knighthood, "without fear and without reproach."

Perhaps there was a real King Arthur, who led the Britons against the Saxon invaders of their land, who was killed by his traitor nephew, and who was buried at Glastonbury,—the valley of Avilion of the legends; perhaps there was a slight historical nucleus around which all the romantic material was crystallising through the centuries, but the Arthur of romance came largely from the imagination of the early writers.

And yet, though our "own ideal knight" may never have trod the soil of Britain or Roman or Saxon England, his chivalrous character and the knightly deeds of his followers are real to us, if we read them rightly, for "the poet's ideal was the truest truth." Though the sacred vessel—the Holy Grail—of the Christ's last supper with His disciples has not been borne about the earth in material form, to be seen only by those of stainless life and character, it is eternally true that the "pure in heart" are "blessed," "for they shall see God." This is what the Quest of the Holy Grail means, and there is still many a true Sir Galahad, who can say, as he did,

"My strength is as the strength of ten, Because my heart is pure,"

and who attains the highest glory of knighthood, as before his clear vision

"down dark tides the glory glides, And starlike mingles with the stars."

We call these beautiful stories of long ago Stories of Chivalry, for, in the Middle Ages, chivalry influenced all that people did and said and thought. It began in the times of Charlemagne, a hundred years before our own King Alfred, and only very gradually it made its way through all the social order. Charlemagne was really a very great man, and because he was so, he left Western Europe a far better place to live in than he found it. Into the social life of his time he brought something like order and justice and peace, and so he greatly helped the Christian Church to do its work of teaching the rough and warlike Franks and Saxons and Normans the gentle ways of thrift and helpfulness.

Charlemagne's "heerban," or call to arms, required that certain of his men should attend him on horseback, and this mounted service was the beginning of what is known as chivalry. The lesser nobles of each feudal chief served their overlords on horseback, *à cheval*, in times of war; they were called *knights*, which originally meant servants,—German *knechte*; and the system of knighthood, its rules, customs, and duties, was called chivalry,—French *chevalerie*.

Chivalry belongs chiefly to the twelfth, thirteenth, and fourteenth centuries,—to about the time between King Richard of the Lion Heart and Prince Hal. There is no trace of ideas peculiar to it in the writings of the old Anglo-Saxons or in the *Nibelungen Lied* of Germany. Geoffrey of Monmouth, who died, it is said, in the year 1154, is about the earliest writer who mentions customs that belong especially to chivalry. The Crusades, of Geoffrey's century and of the one following, gave much opportunity for its growth and practice; but in the fifteenth century chivalrous fashions and fancies began to seem absurd, and later, perhaps partly through the ridicule of that old-time book "Don Quixote," chivalry was finally laughed quite out of existence.

The order of knighthood was given only after years of training and discipline. From his seventh year to his fourteenth the nobleman's son was a *page* at the court or in the castle of his patron, learning the principles of religion, obedience, and gallantry. At fourteen, as a *squire*, the boy began a severer course of training, in order to become skilled in horsemanship, and to gain strength and courage, as well as the refinements and graces necessary in the company of knights and ladies.

Finally, at twenty-one, his training was complete, and with elaborate and solemn formality the *squire* was made a *knight*. Then, after a strict oath to be loyal, courteous, and brave, the armour was buckled on, and the proud young chevalier rode out into the world, strong for good or ill in limb, strong in impenetrable armour, strong in a social custom that lifted him above the common people about him.

When rightly exercised chivalry was a great blessing to the people of its time. It offered high ideals of pure-minded, warm-hearted, courtly, courageous Christian manhood. It did much to arouse thought, to quicken sympathy, to purify morals, to make men truly brave and loyal. Of course this ideal of character was not in the days of chivalry—ideals are not often now—very fully realised. The Mediaeval, like the Modern, abused his power of muscle, of sword, of rank. His liberty as a knight-errant sometimes descended into the licence of a highwayman; his pride in the opportunity for helpfulness grew to be the braggadocio of a bully; his freedom of personal choice became the insolence of lawlessness; his pretended purity and justice proved wanton selfishness.

Because of these abuses that crept into the system, it is well for the world that gunpowder at last came, to break through the knight's coat of mail, to teach the nobility respect for common men, roughly to end this age of so much superficial politeness and savage bravery, and to bring in a more democratic social order.

The books of any age are for us a record of how the people of that age thought, how they lived, and what kind of men and women they tried to be. The old romances of chivalry give us clear pictures of the knights and ladies of the Middle Ages, and we shall lose the delight and the profit they may give us, if we think only of the defects of chivalry, and close our eyes to the really worthy motives of those far-off times, and so miss seeing what chivalry was able to do, while it lasted, to make men and women better and happier.

U. Waldo Cutler

Before reading the Arthur stories themselves it is well to know something about the way they have been built up, as one writer after another has taken the material left by predecessors, and has worked into it fresh conceptions of things brave and true. First there was the old Latin chronicle of Nennius, the earliest trace of Arthurian fact or fancy, with a single paragraph given to Arthur and his twelve great battles. This chronicle itself may have been based on yet earlier Welsh stories, which had been passed on, perhaps for centuries, by oral tradition from father to son, and gradually woven together into some legendary history of Oldest England in the local language of Brittany, across the English Channel. This original book is referred to by later writers, but was long ago lost. Geoffrey of Monmouth says it was the source of his material for his "Historia Britonum." Geoffrey's history, in Latin prose, written some time about the middle of the twelfth century, remains as the earliest definite record of the legends connected with King Arthur.

Only a little later Geoffrey's Latin history was translated by Wace and others into Norman French, and here the Arthur material first appeared in verse form. Then, still later in the twelfth century, Walter Map worked the same stories over into French prose, and at the same time put so much of his own knowledge and imagination with them, that we may almost say that he was the maker of the Arthur romances.

Soon after the year twelve hundred,—a half century after Geoffrey of Monmouth first set our English ancestors to thinking about the legendary old hero of the times of the Anglo-Saxon conquest—Layamon, parish priest of Ernly, in Worcestershire, gave to the English language (as distinct from the earlier Anglo-Saxon) his poem "Brut." This was a translation and enlargement of Wace's old French poem having Arthur as hero. So these stories of King Arthur, of Welsh or Celtic origin, came through the Latin, and then through French verse and prose, into our own speech, and so began their career down the centuries of our more modern history.

After giving ideas to generation after generation of romance writers of many countries and in many languages, these same romantic stories were, in the fifteenth century, skilfully brought together into one connected prose narrative,—one of the choicest of the older English classics, "Le Morte Darthur," by Sir Thomas Malory. Those were troublous times when Sir Thomas, perhaps after having himself fought and suffered in the Wars of the Roses then in progress, found some quiet spot in Warwickshire in which to put together in lasting form the fine old stories that already in his day were classics.

Malory finished his book in 1470, and its permanence for all time was assured fifteen years later, when Caxton, after the "symple connynge" that God had sent him (to use the quaint forms of expression then common), "under the favour and correctyon of al noble lordes and gentylmen emprysed to emprynte a book of the noble hystoryes of the sayd Kynge Arthur and of certeyn of his knyghtes after a copye unto him delyuerd whyche copye Syr Thomas Malorye dyd take oute of certeyn bookes of Frensche and reduced it in to Englysche." This hard-headed business man,—this fifteenth-century publisher,—was rather doubtful about the Briton king of a thousand years before his day, and to those urging upon him the venture of printing Malory's book he answered: "Dyuers men holde oppynyon that there was no suche Arthur and that alle suche bookes as been maad of hym ben fayned and fables by cause that somme cronycles make of him no mencyon ne remember him noo thynge ne of his knyghtes."

But the arguments of those in favour of the undertaking prevailed, greatly to the advantage of the four centuries that have followed, during which "Le Morte Darthur" has been a constant source of poetic inspiration. Generation after generation of readers and of writers have drawn life from its chapters, and the new delight in Tennyson's "Idylls of the King," almost of our own time, shows that the fountain has not yet been drained dry.

Malory's "Morte Darthur" is a long book, and its really great interest is partly hidden from us by forms of expression that belong only to the time when it was first written. Besides this, the ideas of what was right and proper in conduct and speech—moral standards—were far lower in Malory's day than they are now.

The purpose of this new little volume is to bring the old tales freshly to the attention of young people of the present time. It keeps, as far as may be, the exact language and the spirit of the original, chooses such stories as best represent the whole, and modifies these only in order to remove what could possibly hide the thought, or be so crude in taste and morals as to seem unworthy of the really high-minded author of five hundred years ago. It aims also so to condense the book that, in this age of hurry, readers may not be repelled from the tales merely because of their length.

Chivalry of just King Arthur's kind was given up long ago, but that for which it stood—human fellowship in noble purpose—is far older than the institution of knighthood or than even the traditions of the energetic, brave, true, helpful King Arthur himself. It links us with all the past and all the future. The knights of the twentieth century do not set out in chain-armour to right the wrongs of the oppressed by force of arms, but the best influences of chivalry have been preserved for the quickening of a broader and a nobler world than was ever in the dreams of knight-errant of old. Modern heroes of the genuine type owe more than they know to those of Arthur's court who swore:

"To reverence the King, as if he were Their conscience, and their conscience as their King, To break the heathen and uphold the Christ, To ride abroad redressing human wrongs, To speak no slander, no, nor listen to it, To honour his own word as if his God's, To lead sweet lives in purest chastity, To love one maiden only, cleave to her, And worship her by years of noble deeds, Until they won her."

"Antiquity produced heroes, but not gentlemen," someone has said. In the days of Charlemagne and Alfred began the training which, continued in the days of Chaucer and Sir Thomas Malory and many, many more, has given to this our age that highest type of manhood, the Christian gentleman.

U. W. C.

Of the Birth of King Arthur

It befell in the days of Uther Pendragon, when he was king of all England, that there was a mighty duke in Cornwall that held war against him a long time. And the duke was named the Duke of Tintagil. Ten miles away from his castle, called Terrabil, there was, in the castle Tintagil, Igraine of Cornwall, that King Uther liked and loved well, for she was a good and fair lady, and passing wise. He made her great cheer out of measure, and desired to have her love in return; but she would not assent unto him, and for pure anger and for great love of fair Igraine King Uther fell sick.

At that time there lived a powerful magician named Merlin, who could appear in any place he chose, could change his looks as he liked, and at will could do wonderful things to help or to harm knights and ladies. So to King Uther came Sir Ulfius, a noble knight, and said, "I will seek Merlin, and he shall do you remedy so that your heart shall be pleased." So Ulfius departed, and by adventure met Merlin in beggar's array, and made him promise to be not long behind in riding to Uther's pavilion.

Soon Merlin stood by the king's side and said: "I know all your heart, and promise ye shall have your desire, if ye will be sworn to fulfil my wish." This the king solemnly agreed to do, and then Merlin said: "After ye shall win Igraine as wife, a child shall be born to you that is to be given unto me to be brought up as I will; this shall be for your honour and the child's avail."

That night King Uther met in battle the Duke of Tintagil, who had protected Igraine in her castle, and overcame him. Then Igraine welcomed Uther as her true lover, for Merlin had given him the appearance of one dear to her, and, the barons being all well accorded, the two were married on a morning with great mirth and joy.

When the time came that Igraine should bear a son, Merlin came again unto the King to claim his promise, and he said: "I know a lord of yours in this land, a passing true man and a faithful, named Sir Ector, and he shall have the nourishing of your child. Let the young Prince be delivered to me at yonder privy postern, when I come for him."

So the babe, Arthur Pendragon, bound in a cloth of gold, was taken by two knights and two ladies to the postern gate of the castle and delivered unto Merlin, disguised as a poor man, and by him was carried forth to Sir Ector, whose wife nourished him as her own child.

Then within two years King Uther fell sick of a great malady. Wherefore all the barons made great sorrow, and asked Merlin what counsel were best, for few of them had ever seen or heard of the young child, Arthur. On the morn all by Merlin's counsel came before the King, and Merlin said: "Sir, shall your son Arthur be king, after your days, of this realm with all the appurtenance?"

Then Uther Pendragon turned him and said in hearing of them all, "I give him God's blessing and mine, and bid him righteously and honourably to claim the crown upon forfeiture of my blessing."

Therewith he died, and he was buried as befitted a king, and the Queen, fair Igraine, and all the barons made great sorrow.

Uther's Son, Rightwise King of All England

Then stood the kingdom in great jeopardy a long while, for every lord strengthened himself, and many a one thought to be king rather than be ruled by a child that they had never known. All this confusion Merlin had foreseen, and he had taken the young prince away, to keep him safe from the jealous barons until he should be old enough to rule wisely for himself. Even Sir Ector did not know that the boy growing up with his own son Kay was the King's child, and heir to the realm.

When now young Arthur had grown into a tall youth, well trained in all the exercises of honourable knighthood, Merlin went to the Archbishop of Canterbury and counselled him to send to all the lords of the realm and all the gentlemen of arms, that they should come to London at Christmas time, since God of His great mercy would at that time show by miracle who should be rightwise king of the realm. The Archbishop did as Merlin advised, and all the great knights made them clean of their life so that their prayer might be the more acceptable unto God, and when Christmas came they went unto London, each one thinking that perchance his wish to be made king should be granted. So in the greatest church of the city (whether it was St Paul's or not the old chronicle maketh no mention) all were at their prayers long ere day.

When matins were done and they came out of the church, there was seen in the churchyard a great square stone, in the midst of which was an anvil of steel, a foot high, with a fair sword naked at the point sticking through it. Written in gold about the sword were letters that read thus: "Whoso pulleth out this sword from this stone and anvil is rightwise king born of all England."

[Illustration: The Dedication.]

All the people marvelled at the stone and the inscription, and some assayed—such as would be king—to draw out the sword. But none might stir it, and the Archbishop said: "He is not here that shall achieve this sword, but doubt not God will make him known. This now is my counsel, that we cause to be chosen ten knights, men of good fame, to guard this sword until the rightful possessor shall appear."

So it was ordained, and it was proclaimed that every man should assay that would, to win the sword. And upon New Year's Day the barons held jousts and a tournament for all knights that would engage. All this was ordained for to keep the lords and the commons together, for the Archbishop trusted that God would soon make him known that should win the sword. So upon New Year's Day the barons rode to the field, some to joust and some to tourney; and it happened that Sir Ector rode also, and with him Sir Kay, his son, that had just been made knight, and young Arthur that was his foster-brother.

As they rode to the joust-ward Sir Kay suddenly missed his sword, which he had left at his father's lodging, and he begged young Arthur to ride and fetch it. "I will gladly," said Arthur, and he hastened off home. But the lady and all the household were out to see the jousting, and he found nobody at home to deliver him the sword. Then was Arthur troubled, and said to himself, "I will ride to the churchyard and take the sword that sticketh in the stone, for my brother Sir Kay shall not be without a sword this day."

So when he came to the great stone Arthur alighted, and tied his horse to the stile. He then went straight to the tent of the guards, but found no knights there, for they were at the jousting. So he took the sword by the handles, and lightly and fiercely pulled it out of the anvil; then he mounted his horse and rode his way till he came to his brother Sir Kay, and delivered him the sword.

As soon as Sir Kay saw the sword, he knew well it was that one of the stone, and so he rode away to his father, Sir Ector, and said: "Sir, lo here is the sword of the stone; wherefore I must be king of this land."

When Sir Ector beheld the sword, all three returned to the church and entered it. Anon Sir Ector made Sir Kay to swear upon a book how he came by that sword. And Sir Kay answered that Arthur had brought it to him. "And how gat ye the sword?" said he to Arthur; and when Sir Ector heard how it had been pulled from the anvil, he said to Arthur: "Now I understand ye must be king of this land."

"Wherefore I?" said Arthur, "and for what cause?"

"Sir," said Ector, "for God will have it so; for there should never man have drawn out this sword but he that shall be rightwise king. Now let me see whether ye can put the sword there as it was, and pull it out again."

"That is no mastery," said Arthur, and so he put it into the stone. Therewith Sir Ector assayed to pull out the sword, and failed. Then Sir Kay pulled at it with all his might, but it would not yield.

"Now shall ye assay again," said Sir Ector to Arthur.

"I will well," said Arthur, and pulled it out easily a second time.

Now was Sir Ector sure that Arthur was of higher blood than had been thought, and that the rightful king had been made known. And he told his foster-son all, how he was not his father, but had taken him to nourish at Merlin's request. Arthur was grieved indeed when he understood that Sir Ector was not his father, and that the good lady that had fostered and kept him as her own son was not his true mother, and he said to Sir Ector, "If ever it be God's will that I be king, as ye say, ye shall desire of me what I may do, and I shall not fail you."

Therewithal they went unto the Archbishop and told him how the sword was achieved, and by whom. And all the barons came thither, that whoever would might assay to take the sword. But there before them all none might take it out but Arthur. Now many lords became wroth, and said it was great shame unto them all and to the realm to be governed by a boy. They contended so at that time that the matter was put off till Candlemas, when all the barons should meet there again. A pavilion was set over the stone and the sword, and the ten knights were ordained to watch there day and night, five being always on guard.

So at Candlemas many more great lords came thither to win the sword, but none might prevail except Arthur. The barons were sore aggrieved at this, and again put it off in delay till the high feast of Easter. And as Arthur sped afore, so did he at Easter; yet there were some of the great lords that had indignation that Arthur should be their king, and put it off in a delay till the feast of Pentecost.

At the feast of Pentecost all manner of men assayed to pull at the sword, yet none might prevail but Arthur; and he pulled it out afore all the lords and commons that were there. Wherefore all the commons cried at once, "We will have Arthur unto our king; we will put him no more in delay, for we all see that it is God's will that he shall be our king, and who that holdeth against it we will slay as traitor." And they kneeled down all at once, both rich and poor, and begged mercy of Arthur, because they had delayed so long. And Arthur forgave them, and took the sword between both his hands, and offered it upon the altar where the Archbishop was, and so was he made knight of the best man that was there.

And anon was the coronation made, and there Arthur swore unto his lords and the commons to be a true king, to stand for justice all the days of his life. Then he made all the lords that were subject to the crown to come in, and to do service as they ought to do. And many great wrongs that had been done since the death of King Uther were righted, and to lords, knights, ladies, and gentlemen were given back the lands of which they had been unjustly deprived. When the king had thus established justice in all the countries about London, he made Sir Kay seneschal of England, and other officers he appointed also that should aid in keeping back his enemies and holding his realm in peace and orderliness.

How Arthur Gat His Sword Excalibur

On a day there came into the court of the young King a squire on horseback, bringing a knight, his master, mortally wounded, and seeking justice against the murderer. Then came up Griflet, that was but a squire, a young man of the age of King Arthur, and asked to be given the order of knighthood, that he might ride out against the knight that had done the evil deed, who dwelt by a well in the forest.

Arthur was loath to bring this passing brave youth into peril by giving him so high an adventure; but at the desire of Griflet the King at the last gave him the order of knighthood, and he rode away till he came to the fountain.

There he saw the pavilion of the knight, and his horse all saddled and bridled, and his shield of divers colours, and a great spear hanging on a tree hard by. Griflet struck the shield with the butt of his spear, so that it fell clattering down to the ground. With that the knight came out of the pavilion and said, "Fair knight, why smote ye down my shield?"

"For I will joust with you," said Griflet.

"It is better ye do not," said the knight, "for ye are but a young and late-made knight, and your might is nothing to mine."

But Griflet would have it so, and the two ran together with such force that Griflet's spear was all shattered, and horse and rider fell down sore wounded. When the knight saw the youth lying on the ground, he was heavy of heart; and he unlaced his helm to give him air, and finally setting him on his horse, sent him with cheering words back to the court. Here great dole was made for him because of his wounds, and Arthur was passing wroth for the hurt of Sir Griflet.

The next morning ere day the King ordered his best horse, and in full armour rode out alone to encounter the knight of the fountain. It was a strong battle they had. Arthur's spear was all shattered, and his horse fell to the ground. Then they fought with swords with many great strokes and much blood-shed on both sides. Finally by a mighty blow from his enemy,—a passing big man of might,—Arthur's sword was smitten in two pieces, and he was called upon to yield himself as overcome and recreant, or die.

"As for death," said King Arthur, "welcome be it when it cometh; but to yield me unto thee as recreant, I had rather die than to be so shamed."

Therewithal came Merlin, and made known who Arthur was. Then by enchantment he caused the knight to fall into a deep sleep, and bore Arthur away to a hermit to be cured of his wounds.

When, after three days of rest and healing, he was riding with Merlin through the forest, King Arthur said, "I have no sword."

"No matter," said Merlin; "there is one near by that I can perhaps get for you."

So they rode on till it chanced that they passed a fair and broad lake. In the midst of the water Arthur became aware of an arm clothed in white samite holding aloft a beautiful sword.

"Lo! there is the sword of which I spake," said Merlin, "and yonder is the Lady of the Lake ready to help you to it, if ye speak fair to her."

Anon came the damsel unto Arthur and saluted him, and he her again. "Damsel," said Arthur, "what sword is it that the arm holdeth above the water yonder? I would it were mine, for I have no sword."

"Sir Arthur King," said the damsel, "that sword is mine, and if ye will give me a gift when I ask it you, go ye into yonder barge and row yourself to the sword, and take it and the scabbard with you."

So Sir Arthur and Merlin alighted and tied their horses to a tree, and then they went into the magic boat. Soon they were beside the sword that the hand held up. Arthur took it by the handle, the arm and the hand went down beneath the water, and the two travellers rowed back to the land and went forth.

As they rode along Arthur looked on the sword, which had the name Excalibur, that is as much as to say Cut-steel, and he liked it passing well, for the handle was all set with precious stones.

"Which like you better," said Merlin, "the sword or the scabbard?"

"The sword," replied Arthur.

"Ye are unwise," said Merlin; "the scabbard is worth ten of the sword, for while ye have the scabbard upon you, ye shall lose no blood; therefore keep well the scabbard always with you."

In this way Arthur came by Excalibur, and many an adventure he was to have with it, and was to suffer great danger when by evil interference it was, as we shall see, for a time stolen from him. With it in hand the hardest fight went well in the end, for the scabbard kept him from weakness, and a mysterious power lay in the strong, true blade that none could withstand, until the time came for King Arthur to give back the sword to the Lady of the Lake and to die of the wounds of a traitor.

So King Arthur and Merlin rode on, and when they came back safe to Carlion and the court the knights were passing glad. Some wondered that the king would risk himself abroad so alone, but all men of valour said it was merry to be under such a chief that would put his person in adventure as other poor knights did.

BALIN AND BALAN

On a day there came a messenger to King Arthur saying that King Ryons of North Wales, a strong man in body, and passing proud, had discomfited and overcome eleven kings, and each of these to do him homage had cut his beard clean off as trimming for King Ryons' royal mantle. One place of the mantle still lacked trimming; wherefore he sent for Arthur's beard, and if he did not receive it he would enter England to burn and slay, and never would he leave till he had Arthur, head and all.

"Well," said Arthur to the messenger, "thou hast said thy message, the most insolent ever sent unto a king. Thou seest my beard is full young yet to make a trimming of it. Tell thou thy king I owe him no homage, but ere long he shall do me homage on both his knees." So the messenger departed.

Among those who, at Arthur's call, gathered at Camelot to withstand King Ryons' invasion of the land was a knight that had been Arthur's prisoner half a year and more for some wrong done to one of the court. The name of this knight was Balin, a strong, courageous man, but poor and so poorly clothed that he was thought to be of no honour. But worthiness and good deeds are not all only in arrayment. Manhood and honour is hid within man's person, and many an honourable knight is not known unto all people through his clothing. This Balin felt deeply the insult of King Ryons, and anon armed himself to ride forth to meet with him and mayhap to destroy him, in the hope that then King Arthur would again be his good and gracious lord.

The meanwhile that this knight was making ready to depart on this adventure, there came to Arthur's court the Lady of the Lake, and she now asked of him the gift that he promised her when she gave him his sword Excalibur.

"Ask what ye will," said the King, "and ye shall have it, if it lie in my power to give."

Thereupon she demanded Balin's head, and would take none other thing.

"Truly," said King Arthur, "I may not grant this with my honour," and Balin was allowed to make ready for the adventure with King Ryons.

But ere he had left the court he saw the Lady of the Lake. He went straight to her, and with his sword lightly smote off her head before King Arthur, for he knew her as the untruest lady living, one that by enchantment and sorcery had been the destroyer of many good knights.

"Alas! for shame," said Arthur. "Why have ye done so? Ye have shamed me and all my court, for this was a lady that I was beholden to, and hither she came under my safe conduct. I shall never forgive you that trespass. What cause soever ye had, ye should have spared her in my presence; therefore withdraw you out of my court in all haste that ye may."

So Balin,—called Balin the Wild for his savage and reckless nature,—departed with his squire, and King Arthur and all the court made great mourning, and had shame at the death of the Lady of the Lake. Then the King buried her richly.

In sorrow over the evil he had wrought and the disfavour of his king, Balin turned his horse towards a great forest, and there by the armour he was ware of his brother Balan. And when they were met, they put off their helms and kissed together, and wept for joy.

Anon the knight Balin told his brother of the death of the Lady of the Lake, and said: "Truly I am right heavy of heart that my lord Arthur is displeased with me, for he is the most honourable knight that reigneth on earth, and his love I will get or else I will put my life in adventure with King Ryons, that lieth now at the castle Terrabil. Thither will we ride together in all haste, to prove our honour and prowess upon him."

"I will gladly do that," said Balan; "we will help each other as brothers ought to do."

So they took their way to find King Ryons, and as they rode along together they encountered him in a straight way with threescore knights. Anon Balin and Balan smote him down from his horse, and slew on the right hand and the left hand more than forty of his men. The remnant fled, and King Ryons yielded him unto their grace as prisoner. So they laid him on a horse-litter, for he was fiercely wounded, and brought him to Camelot. There they delivered him to the porters and charged them with him; and then they two returned to further adventure.

And Balin rode towards the castle of King Pellam to revenge the wrongs of knights and ladies on a treacherous knight named Garlon. He had a fifteen days' journey thither, and the day he came unto the castle there began a great feast. Balin was well received, and led to a chamber, where he laid off his armour. They also brought him robes to his pleasure, and would have had him leave his sword behind him.

"Nay," said Balin, "that do I not, for it is the custom of my country for a knight always to have his weapon with him, and that custom will I keep, or else I will depart as I came."

Then they gave him leave to wear his sword, and so he went unto the hall and was set among the knights of honour.

Soon he saw the false knight Garlon, and thought to himself: "If I slay him here I shall not escape, and if I leave him now, peradventure I shall never meet with him again at such a good time, and much harm will he do if he live."

Then this Garlon espied that Balin watched him, and he came and smote Balin on the face, and said: "Knight, why watchest thou me so? Eat thy meat, and do that thou camest for."

Then Balin said, "I will do that I came for," and rose up fiercely and clove his head to the shoulders.

Anon all the knights arose from the table to set on Balin, and King Pellam himself caught in his hand a grim weapon and smote eagerly at Balin, but Balin put his sword betwixt his head and the stroke. With that his sword was broken in sunder, and he, now weaponless, ran into the chamber to seek some weapon, and so, from chamber to chamber, but no weapon could he find, and alway King Pellam came after him.

At last Balin entered into a chamber that was marvellously well furnished and richly, wherein was a bed arrayed with cloth of gold, the richest that might be thought, and thereby a table of clean gold, and upon the table a marvellous spear, strangely wrought. And when Balin saw that spear he took it in his hand, and turned to King Pellam and smote him passing hard with it so that he fell down in a swoon. Therewith the castle roof and walls brake and fell to the earth, and Balin also, so that he might not stir foot nor hand, for through that dolorous stroke the most part of the castle that was fallen down lay upon him and Pellam.

After three days Merlin came thither, and he took up Balin and gat him a good horse, for his was dead, and bade him ride out of the country. Merlin also told him that his stroke had turned to great dole, trouble, and grief, for the marvellous spear was the same with which Longius, the Roman soldier, smote our Lord Jesus Christ to the heart at the crucifixion.

Then departed Balin from Merlin, never to meet him again, and rode forth through the fair countries and cities about Pellam Castle, and found people dead, slain on every side. And all that were left alive cried: "O Balin, thou hast caused great damage in these countries, for by the dolorous stroke thou gavest unto King Pellam three countries are destroyed, and doubt not but the vengeance will fall on thee at the last."

When Balin was out of those countries he was passing glad, and after many days he came by a cross, whereon were letters of gold written that said, "It is not for any knight alone to ride towards this castle." Then saw he an old hoary gentleman coming towards him that said, "Balin the Wild, thou passest thy bounds to come this way; therefore turn again and it will avail thee." The old gentleman vanished away, and then Balin heard a horn blow, as if for the death of a beast in the chase. "That blast," said he, "is blown for me, for I am the prize, yet am I not dead." Anon he saw a hundred ladies and many knights, that welcomed him with fair semblance, and made him passing good cheer seemingly, and led him into the castle, where there were dancing and minstrelsy, and all manner of joy.

Then the chief lady of the castle said, "Knight, you must have ado with a knight close by that keepeth an island, for there may no man pass this way but he must joust, ere he go farther."

"That is an unhappy custom," said Balin, "that a knight may not pass this way unless he joust, but since that is my duty, thereto am I ready. Travelling men are oft weary, and their horses also; but though my horse be weary my heart is not weary."

"Sir," said the knight then to Balin, "me thinketh your shield is not good; I will lend you a better."

So Balin took the shield that was unknown, and left his own, and rode unto the island. He put himself and his horse in a great boat, and when he came on the other side he met with a damsel, and she said, "O Knight Balin, why hast thou left thine own shield? Alas! thou hast put thyself in great danger, for by thine own shield thou shouldst have been known. It is a great pity, for of thy prowess and hardiness thou hast no equal living."

"Me repenteth," said Balin, "that ever I came within this country, but I may not turn now again for shame, and what adventure shall fall to me, be it life or death, I will take the adventure that shall come to me."

Then he looked on his armour, and understood he was well armed, for which he was thankful, and so he mounted upon his horse. Then before him he saw come riding out of a castle a knight in red armour, and his horse was all trapped in the same colour. When this knight in red beheld Balin, he thought he was like his brother; but because he knew not his shield, he deemed it was not he. And so they couched their spears and came marvellously fast together, and they smote each other in the shields; but their spears were so heavy and their course so swift that horse and man were borne down, and both knights lay in a swoon. Balin was bruised sore with the fall of his horse, for he was weary with travel, and Balan (for the knight in red was none other) was the first that rose to his feet. He drew his sword and went towards Balin, who arose and went against him. But Balan smote Balin first, striking through his shield and cleaving his helm. Then Balin smote him in return with that unhappy sword that had already wrought so great harm, and the blow well nigh felled his brother Balan. So they fought there together till their breaths failed.

Then Balin looked up to the castle, and saw the towers stand full of ladies; so they went to battle again and wounded each other dolefully. Then they breathed ofttimes, and yet again went unto battle, until all the place there was blood-red from the great wounds that either had smitten other, and their hauberks became unriveted so that naked they were on every side.

At last Balan, the younger brother, withdrew a little and laid himself down. Then said Balin the Wild, "What knight art thou? for ere now I found never a knight that matched me."

"My name is," said he, "Balan, brother to the good knight Balin."

"Alas!" said Balin, "that ever I should see this day." Thereupon he fell backward in a swoon.

Then Balan crept on all fours to his brother and put oft his helm, but he might not know him, his visage was so disguised by blood and wounds. But when Balin awoke, he said, "O Balan, my brother, thou hast slain me and I thee, wherefore all the wide world shall speak of us both."

"Alas!" said Balan; "that ever I saw this day, that through mishap I might not know thee! Because thou hadst another shield I deemed thou wert another knight."

"Alas!" said Balin, "all this was caused by an unhappy knight in the castle, that made me leave mine own shield, to the destruction of us both."

Then anon Balan died, and at midnight after, Balin; so both were buried together, and the lady of the castle had Balan's name written on the tomb and how he was there slain by his brother's hand, but she knew not Balin's name. In the morn came Merlin and wrote Balin's inscription also in letters of gold: "Here lieth Balin the Wild, that smote the dolorous stroke."

Soon after this was done Merlin came to King Arthur and told him of the dolorous stroke that Balin gave King Pellam, and how Balin and Balan fought together the most marvellous battle that ever was heard of, and how they buried both in one tomb. "Alas!" said King Arthur; "this is the greatest pity that ever I heard tell of two knights, for in the world I know not such two knights."

Thus endeth the tale of Balin and Balan, two brethren born in Northumberland, good knights both.

The Noble Order of the Round Table

Arthur was indeed king, but enemies long held out against his just authority. When he went into Wales to be crowned at the city of Carlion, he let cry a great feast to be holden at Pentecost. Unto this feast came the six kings of that region with many of their knights, and Arthur thought it was to do him honour. But when he made joy of their coming and sent them great presents, the kings would none receive, and said they had no joy to receive gifts of a beardless boy that was come of low birth. They sent him word that they were come to give him gifts with hard swords betwixt the neck and the shoulders, for it was great shame to all of them to see such a boy have rule of so noble a realm as this land was.

This answer was told King Arthur, who now betook himself to a strong tower and five hundred good men with him. Here the six kings laid siege to him, but he was well victualled; and soon Merlin came and bade him fear not, but speak boldly to his enemies, "for," said he, "ye shall overcome them all, whether they will or nill."

So the King armed himself and all his knights and came out to do battle with his enemies. Then three hundred good men of the best that were with the kings went straight over unto King Arthur, which comforted him greatly. So he set upon the hosts of the six kings, and he and his men did marvellous deeds of arms. Therewith he put them back, and then the commons of Carlion arose with clubs and staves and slew many of the enemy, and so they fled away.

Since the enemy were still passing strong, Merlin counselled King Arthur to send letters well devised beyond the sea to the two brethren, marvellous good men of their hands, named one King Ban of Benwick and the other King Bors of Gaul, and to say to them that, if they would come and help King Arthur in his wars, he in turn would be sworn unto them to help them in their wars against King Claudas, a mighty man that strove with them for a castle.

So there were made letters in the pleasantest wise, according to King Arthur's desire, and Ulfius and Brastias, the messengers, rode forth well horsed and well armed, and so passed the sea and came to the city of Benwick. Here they had good cheer as long as they tarried, and received the answer that King Ban and King Bors would come unto King Arthur in all the haste they might.

Now those six kings in Wales had by their means gotten unto them five other kings, and all swore together that for weal or woe they would not leave each other till they had destroyed Arthur. So their whole host drew towards Arthur, now strengthened by Ban and Bors with their followers that had crossed from Gaul to his aid. Then followed a great battle, and they did on both sides great deeds of arms until at the last Merlin counselled Arthur to fight no longer, since the eleven kings had more on hand than they were ware of, and would soon depart home; for a messenger would come and tell them that lawless people as well as Saracens, forty thousand in number, had entered their lands and were burning and slaying without mercy. So the great battle was ended, and the eleven kings went to their own country.

Now King Arthur, King Ban, and King Bors came with their following into the country of Cameliard, and there aided King Leodegrance against an enemy of that land. King Leodegrance thanked them for their goodness, and made them great cheer ere King Ban and King Bors departed back towards Benwick.

In Cameliard Arthur had the first sight of Guenever, the King's daughter, and ever afterwards he loved her. So when peace was once more in his land, King Arthur asked counsel of Merlin about seeking her as his wife, for to him she was the most valiant and fairest lady living or to be found.

"Sir," said Merlin, "as for her beauty, she is one of the fairest alive, but if ye loved her not so well as ye do, I could choose better for you. Yet when a man's heart is set, he will be loath to change."

So Merlin was sent forth to King Leodegrance, and he told him of King Arthur's desire. King Leodegrance was glad that so worthy a king of prowess and of nobleness would wed his daughter, and promised him as wedding gift,—not lands, for he had enough and needed none,—but what would please him much more, the Table Round, which Uther Pendragon had given to the King of Cameliard,—a table made by Merlin at which an hundred and fifty knights might be seated.

So Guenever, attended by Merlin and an hundred good knights (all King Leodegrance could spare, so many had been slain in his wars) with the

Round Table rode with great pomp by water and by land to London. There King Arthur made great joy of their coming, for he had long loved Guenever. Also the gift pleased him more than right great riches. And the marriage and the coronation were ordained with all speed in the most honourable wise that could be devised.

Merlin was sent to espy out in all the land fifty knights of most prowess and honour, who should make up the full number for the Round Table. Only twenty-eight could he find worthy enough, and these Merlin fetched to Arthur's court. And Merlin made sieges (seats), an hundred and fifty in all, for the knights, and he placed in every knight's siege his name in letters of gold.

On that same day King Arthur founded the great order of the Round Table, the fame of which was to last for all time. An hundred and twenty-eight were then sworn as Knights of the Table Round, and every year at the high feast of Pentecost others were to be added as they showed themselves worthy. Only one siege was long empty, the Siege Perilous, for no man should sit therein but one, and if any one of unworthy life were so hardy as to sit therein, he should be destroyed.

With great ceremony each one took the vows of true knighthood, solemnly promising to do no wicked deed, to be loyal to the King, to give mercy to those asking it, always to be courteous and helpful to ladies, and to fight in no wrongful quarrel for wordly gain, upon pain of death or forfeiture of knighthood and King Arthur's favour. Unto this were all the knights of the Round Table sworn, both old and young. To dishonour knighthood was the greatest disgrace; to prove themselves worthy of knightly honour by strong, brave, courteous, loyal bearing under great difficulties was the highest end of living.

So King Arthur stablished all his knights, and to them that were not rich he gave lands; and they rode abroad to right the wrongs of men, and to give help to the oppressed. With their aid he secured order and justice throughout his realm, and then the weakest man might do his work in peace, and prosper.

The Ladies' Knight

The King was wedded unto Dame Guenever at Camelot with great solemnity. Just as all were sitting at the high feast that followed the marriage, there came running into the hall a white hart, followed by a whole pack of hounds with a great cry, and the hart went about the Table Round. At a fierce bite from one of the dogs the hart made a great leap, and overthrew a knight that sat at the table, and so passed forth out of the hall again, with all the dogs after him. When they were gone the King was glad, for they made such a noise, but Merlin said, "Ye may not leave this adventure so lightly. Let call Sir Gawaine, for he must bring again the white hart."

"I will," said the King, "that all be done by your advice." So Sir Gawaine was called, and he took his charge and armed himself for the adventure. Sir Gawaine was one of King Arthur's nephews, and had just been made a knight, for he had asked of the King the gift of knighthood on the same day that he should wed fair Guenever.

So Sir Gawaine rode quickly forth, and Gaheris his brother rode with him, instead of a squire, to do him service. As they followed the hart by the cry of the hounds, they came to a great river. The hart swam over, and they followed after, and so at length they chased him into a castle, where in the chief courtyard the dogs slew the hart before Sir Gawaine and young Gaheris came up. Right so there came a knight out of a room, with a sword drawn in his hand, and he slew two of the greyhounds even in the sight of Sir Gawaine, and the remnant he chased with his sword out of the castle.

When he came back he said, "O my white hart, me repenteth that thou art dead, for my sovereign lady gave thee to me, and poorly have I kept thee. Thy death shall be dear bought, if I live."

Anon he came fiercely towards Sir Gawaine, and they struck mightily together. They clove their shields and broke their helms and hauberks so that the blood ran down to their feet. At the last Sir Gawaine smote the knight so hard that he fell to the earth; and then he cried for mercy and yielded himself, and besought Sir Gawaine as he was a knight and gentleman to save his life.

"Thou shalt die," said Sir Gawaine, "for slaying of my hounds."

"I will make amends," said the knight, "unto my power."

Sir Gawaine would no mercy have, but unlaced his helm to strike off his head, when at that instant came his lady out of a chamber. She fell upon her husband just as the blow descended, and so Sir Gawaine smote off her head by misadventure, and the knight was saved.

"Alas!" said Gaheris, "that is foul and shamefully done; that shame shall never depart from you. Ye should give mercy unto them that ask mercy, for a knight without mercy is without honour."

Sir Gawaine was so astonished at the death of the fair lady that he knew not what he did, and he said unto the knight, "Arise, I will give thee mercy; and go thou unto King Arthur, and tell him how thou art overcome by the knight that went in the quest of the white hart."

"I care not for mercy now," said the knight, "for thou hast slain my lady that I loved best of all earthly things it matters not whether I live or die."

Then Sir Gawaine went into the castle and made ready to rest there all night.

"What will ye do?" said Gaheris; "will ye unarm you in this country? Ye may believe ye have many enemies here."

He had no sooner said that word than there came four knights well armed, and anon they made Sir Gawaine and Gaheris yield themselves as prisoners, in spite of the brave battle wherein Sir Gawaine was sore wounded in the arm.

Early on the morrow there came to Sir Gawaine in the prison one of the ladies of the castle, and said, "Sir Knight, what cheer?"

"Not good," said he.

"It is your own fault," said the lady, "for ye have done a passing foul deed in the slaying of the lady, which will be great disgrace unto you. Be ye not of King Arthur's kin?"

"Yes, truly," said Sir Gawaine. "My name is Gawaine, and my mother is King Arthur's sister."

"Ah, then are ye nephew unto King Arthur," said the lady, "and I shall so speak for you that ye shall have conduct to King Arthur, for love of him."

Then anon they delivered Sir Gawaine under this promise, that he should bear the dead lady to the court, the severed head hanging about his neck. Right so he rode forth unto Camelot, and Merlin made him tell of his adventure, and how he slew the lady, and how he would give no mercy unto the knight, whereby the lady was slain. Then the King and the Queen were greatly displeased with Sir Gawaine, and by ordinance of the Queen there was set a quest of ladies on Sir Gawaine, and they ordered him for ever while he lived to be with all ladies, and to fight for their quarrels; and that ever he should be courteous, and never refuse mercy to him that asketh mercy. Thus was Gawaine sworn upon the four Evangelists that he should never be against lady nor gentlewoman, except if he fought for a lady and his adversary fought for another.

Thus endeth the adventure of Sir Gawaine, that he did at the marriage of King Arthur.

Wise Merlin's Foolishness

Arthur was now established as king over all the land. The great council hall at Camelot, that is Winchester, had been built, some say by Merlin's skill; and the most loyal and the bravest knights of the world had been gathered at Arthur's court to do honour to him and his fair Queen Guenever.

Merlin was Arthur's wisest helper and most powerful friend, as he had before been the helper and friend of his father Uther, for whom he had made the Round Table, signifying the roundness of the world. We have seen how he hid the young Arthur away from the jealousy of the wild barons, and how, by his power over men and his knowledge of what would be, he had saved the King's life and guided his wise rule. The old magician Bleise, that dwelt in Northumberland, was Merlin's master, and he it was that wrote down all the battles of Arthur with his enemies word by word as Merlin told him, and all the battles that were done in Arthur's days, until Merlin was lost, as we shall see, through his own foolishness.

On a time Merlin told King Arthur that he should not endure long, but for all his crafts he should be put in the earth alive. Also he told many things that should befall, and how the king would miss him, so that rather than all his lands he would wish to have him again.

"Ah," said King Arthur, "since ye know of this, provide against it, and put away by your crafts that misadventure."

"Nay," said Merlin, "it cannot be done." For Merlin, now grown an old man in his dotage, had fallen under the spell of a damsel of the court named Nimue. With her he soon departed from the King, and evermore went with her wheresoever she went. Ofttimes he wished to break away from her, but he was so held that he could not be out of her presence. Ever she made him good cheer, till she had learned from him all she desired of his secret craft, and had made him swear that he would never do any enchantment upon her.

[Illustration: Merlin and Nimue]

They went together over the sea unto the land of Benwick, where Ban was king, that had helped Arthur against his enemies. Here Merlin saw young Launcelot, King Ban's son, and he told the queen that this same child should grow to be a man of great honour, so that all Christendom should speak of his prowess. So the queen was comforted of her great sorrow that she made for the mortal war that King Claudas waged on her lord and on her lands.

Then afterwards Nimue and Merlin departed into Cornwall, and by the way he showed her many wonders, and wearied her with his desire for her love. She would fain have been delivered of him, for she was afraid of him, almost believing him a devil's son, and yet she could not put him away by any means.

And so on a time it happened that Merlin showed to her a wonderful cavern in the cliff, closed by an enchanted stone. By her subtle working she soon made Merlin remove the stone and go into the cavern to let her know of the marvels there. Then she so wrought through the magic he had taught her that the stone was placed back again, so that he never came out for all the craft that he could do. And then she departed and left him there.

On a day a certain knight rode to see adventures, and happened to come to the rock where Nimue had put Merlin, and there he heard him make great lamentation. The knight would gladly have helped him, and tried to move the great stone; but it was so heavy that a hundred men might not lift it up. When Merlin knew that the knight sought his deliverance, he bade him leave his labour, for all was in vain. He could never be helped but by her that put him there.

So Merlin's prophecy of his own end was fulfilled, and he passed from the world of men. Arthur truly missed his old friend and marvelled what had become of him. Afterwards, when the last great battle came, he would have given everything to have Merlin with him again, but it could not be.

A Stag-Hunt and What Came of it

It befell that Arthur and many of his knights rode on hunting into a deep forest, and King Arthur, King Uriens of Gore that was the husband of Arthur's sister Morgan le Fay, and Sir Accolon of Gaul followed a great hart so fast that within a while they were ten miles from their fellowship. At the last they chased so sore that they slew their horses underneath them. Then were they all three on foot, and ever they saw the hart afore them passing weary and hard bestead[1]. "Let us go on foot," said King Uriens, "till we meet with some lodging."

Then were they ware of the hart that lay on a great water bank, and a dog biting on his throat, and more other hounds came after. King Arthur now blew the prize[2] and dight[3] the hart.

But the three knights were in sore straits, so far from home, and without horses, and they began to look about the world. Then Arthur saw afore him in a great lake a little ship, all apparelled with silk down to the water, coming right unto them, and it landed on the sands. They went on board, all three, to see what was in the ship. Soon it was dark night, and there suddenly were about them an hundred torches set upon all the sides of the ship boards, and it gave great light.

Therewithal there came out twelve fair damsels, and they set forth for the knights a supper of all meats that they could think. Then they showed them richly beseen[4] chambers for the night, where the three huntsmen slept marvellously. But when they awoke next morning, everything had been changed through the sorcery of Morgan le Fay, that was secretly plotting against her brother, to destroy him. King Uriens awoke in his own bed in Camelot, and Arthur found himself in a dark prison, with many woeful knights complaining about him, and they soon told him for what cause they were there.

The lord of the castle where they were prisoners was the falsest knight alive, a treacherous, cowardly man, named Sir Damas. He had a younger brother, Sir Ontzlake, a good knight of prowess, well beloved of all people, from whom he was keeping back unjustly a full fair manor. Great war had been betwixt these brothers. Ontzlake was a far better fighter than the cowardly Damas, and yet he could not bring the elder to give over the younger brother's inheritance. He offered to fight for it, and wished Sir Damas to find a knight to fight in his stead, if he himself dared not engage. But Sir Damas was so hated that there was never one would fight for him, though he had by force taken all the knights of that whole region and brought them to his prison for to make them willing to take up his cause. Many had died there, and the twenty that were yet alive were lean and spent with hunger, but no one of them would stand against Sir Ontzlake.

Anon there came a damsel unto Arthur and asked him, "What cheer?" "I cannot say," said he. "Sir," said she, "if ye will fight for my lord, ye shall be delivered out of prison, and else ye escape never with life."

"Now," said Arthur, "that is hard, yet had I liefer to fight with a knight than to die in prison," and so it was agreed that he should do the battle on this covenant, that he should be delivered and all the prisoners. With that all the twenty knights were brought out of the dark prison into the hall, and set free, but they all abode to see the battle.

Now turn we unto Accolon of Gaul, that was with King Arthur and King Uriens on the stag-hunt and that fell asleep on the magic ship. When he awoke he found himself beside a deep well, within half a foot of its edge, in great peril of death.

"Heaven save my lord King Arthur and King Uriens," said he, "for these damsels in the ship have betrayed us. They were devils and no women, and if I may escape this misadventure, I shall destroy all false damsels that use enchantments, wherever I may find them."

Right then there came a dwarf with a great mouth and a flat nose, and saluted Sir Accolon and said he came from Queen Morgan le Fay. "She greeteth you well," said he, "and biddeth you be of strong heart, for ye shall fight to-morn with a knight at the hour of prime, and therefore she hath sent you here Excalibur, Arthur's sword, and the scabbard, and she biddeth you as ye love her, that ye do the battle to the uttermost without any mercy, like as ye promised her when ye spake together in private."

Sir Accolon believed he fully understood the message, and he said he should keep his promise now that he had the sword. Just then a knight, who was no other than Sir Ontzlake himself, with a lady and six squires, came up on horseback, saluted Sir Accolon, and begged him to come and rest himself at his manor. So Accolon mounted upon a spare horse and rode to the manor, where he had passing good cheer.

Meantime Sir Damas sent to his brother, Sir Ontzlake, and bade him make ready to fight the next day with a good knight who had agreed to do battle for the disputed heritage; and it happened through Morgan le Fay's trickery that Accolon was lodged with Sir Ontzlake at the very time when this message came. Now Sir Ontzlake was sore troubled at the message, for he had been wounded in both thighs by a spear a short time before, and was suffering much. Still, wounded as he was, he would have taken the battle in hand, had not Sir Accolon offered to fight in his stead, because Morgan le Fay had sent Excalibur and the sheath for the battle with the knight on the morrow. Then Sir Ontzlake was passing glad, and sent word unto his brother, Sir Damas, that he had a knight who would be ready in the field by to-morrow at the hour of prime.

So it was arranged that Sir Arthur and Sir Accolon, unknown to one another, were to fight over the quarrel of the two brothers. Preparations were made accordingly, and all the knights and commons of the country were there to see the encounter. Just as Arthur was ready upon horseback, there came a damsel from Morgan le Fay bringing unto him a sword like unto Excalibur, and the scabbard, and said: "Morgan le Fay sendeth you here your sword for great love." He thanked her, not knowing that the sword and scabbard were counterfeit, and brittle and false.

They went eagerly to the battle, and gave many great strokes. Sir Accolon had all advantage on his side, for he had the real Excalibur, Morgan le Fay having so ordained that King Arthur should have been slain that day. King Arthur's sword never bit like Sir Accolon's, and almost every stroke Sir Accolon gave wounded sore, so that it was a marvel that Arthur stood. Almost from the first it seemed to him that the sword in Accolon's hand must be Excalibur, but he was so full of knighthood that knightly he endured the pain of the many wounds, and held out as well as he might until his sword brake at the cross and fell in the grass among the blood.

Now he expected to die, but he held up his shield, and lost no ground, nor bated any cheer. All men that beheld him said they never saw knight fight so well as Arthur did, considering the blood that he bled, and they were sorry for him. But Accolon was so bold because of Excalibur that he grew passing hardy, and called upon Arthur to yield himself as recreant.

"Nay," said Sir Arthur, "I may not so, for I have promised to do the battle to the uttermost by the faith of my body while my life lasteth, and therefore I had rather die with honour than live with shame; and if it were possible for me to die an hundred times, I had rather die so oft than yield myself to thee; for, though I lack weapon I shall lack no honour, and if thou slay me weaponless that shall be thy shame."

But Accolon cared not for shame, and would not spare. He gave Arthur such a stroke that he fell nigh to the earth; yet he pressed upon Accolon with his shield, and with the pommel of his sword in his hand gave such a blow that Accolon fell back a little.

Now it chanced that one of the damsels of the court, she that had put Merlin under the stone, had come into the field for love of King Arthur, for she knew how Morgan le Fay had determined that Arthur should be slain; therefore she came to save his life. She saw how full of prowess Arthur was, and grieved that so good a knight should be slain through false treason. So when Accolon gave another blow, the sword Excalibur fell out of his hand to the earth. Arthur lightly leaped to it and got it in his hand, and forthwith knew that it was his own Excalibur. Then he saw the scabbard hanging by Accolon's side, and anon pulling it from him, he threw it off as far as he might throw it. Therewith Sir Arthur rushed upon Accolon with all his might and pulled him to the earth. He then snatched off his helmet for the final blow, and the fierce battle was at an end.

"Slay me ye may well," said Accolon, "if it please you, for ye are the best knight that ever I found, and I see well that God is with you."

But now Sir Arthur thought he must have seen this knight, and asked, "Of what country art thou, and of what court?" And when Sir Accolon told him his name, then he remembered him of his sister, Morgan le Fay, and of the enchantment of the ship. He made Accolon tell how he came by the sword, and then Arthur knew all the plot of his sister and of Accolon to have the King slain and herself made queen.

For the first time Arthur now let Accolon know against whom he had been fighting. The fallen knight cried aloud for mercy, when he learned that he had nearly slain the King, and said to all the knights and men that were then there gathered together, "O lords, this noble knight that I have fought withal, which I sorely repent of, is the best man of prowess, of manhood, and of honour in the world, for it is King Arthur himself, the liege lord of us all, and with mishap and with misadventure have I done this battle with the king and lord in whose power I am." Then all the people fell down on their knees, and called upon King Arthur for mercy, which he forthwith granted.

The King was sorely hurt and Accolon's wounds were even worse. Arthur made haste to settle the quarrel of the brothers Sir Damas and Sir Ontzlake by giving the latter his rights and charging Sir Damas upon pain of death never to distress knights-errant that ride on their adventures, and then was carried off to a near-by abbey, and Sir Accolon with him, to have their wounds searched.

Within four days Sir Accolon died from loss of blood during the fight, but King Arthur was well recovered. When Accolon was dead the King let send him on a horse-bier with six knights unto Camelot and said, "Bear him to my sister Morgan le Fay, and say that I send him to her as a present, and tell her that I have my sword Excalibur again and the scabbard."

So they departed with the body.

[1] Hard bestead: in a bad plight.

[2] Prize: death note.

[3] Dight: dressed.

[4] Beseen: of good appearance.

The Treachery of Morgan Le Fay

The meanwhile Morgan le Fay thought that King Arthur was slain, and that she might now be queen of the land, with Sir Accolon as King. Then came tidings unto her that Accolon was dead and King Arthur had his sword again. When Queen Morgan wist all this she was so sorrowful that near her heart brake, but because she would not it were known, outward she kept her countenance, and made no semblance of sorrow. But well she wist, if she remained till her brother Arthur came thither, there should no gold go for her life. Then she went unto Queen Guenever, and asked her leave to ride into the country.

"Ye may abide," said Queen Guenever, "till your brother the King come home."

"I may not," said Morgan le Fay, "for I have such hasty tidings that I may not tarry."

"Well," said Guenever, "ye may depart when ye will."

So early on the morn, ere it was day, she took her horse and rode all that day and most part of the night, and on the morn by noon she came to the abbey of nuns where lay King Arthur. Knowing he was there, she asked where he was at that time; and they answered how he had laid him in his bed to sleep, for he had had but little rest these three nights.

Then she alighted off her horse, and thought for to steal away Excalibur his sword. So she went straight unto his chamber, and no man durst disobey her commandment. There she found Arthur asleep in his bed, and Excalibur in his right hand naked. When she saw that, she was passing heavy that she might not come by the sword without awaking him, and that she wist well would be her death. Then she took the scabbard, and went her way on horseback.

When the King a woke and missed his scabbard, he was wroth, and he asked who had been there. They said his sister Queen Morgan had been there, and had put the scabbard under her mantle, and was gone.

"Alas," said Arthur, "falsely have ye watched me."

"Sir," said they all, "we durst not disobey your sister's commandment."

"Ah," said the King, "let fetch the best horse that may be found, and bid Sir Ontzlake arm him in all haste, and take another good horse and ride with me."

So anon the King and Ontzlake were well armed, and rode after this lady; and so they came by a cross, and asked a cowherd if there came any lady late riding that way.

"Sir," said the poor man, "right late came a lady riding with forty horses, and to yonder forest she rode."

Then they spurred their horses and followed fast. Within a while Arthur had a sight of Morgan le Fay, and he chased as fast as he might. When she espied him following her, she rode a greater pace through the forest till she came to a plain. She saw she might not escape, wherefore she rode unto a lake thereby, and said, "Whatsoever becometh of me, my brother shall not have this scabbard." And then she let throw the scabbard in the deepest of the water, where it sank anon, for it was heavy of gold and precious stones.

Thereupon Queen Morgan rode into a valley where many great stones were, and when she saw that she must be overtaken, she shaped herself, horse and man, by enchantment, unto great marble stones. Anon came Sir Arthur and Sir Ontzlake, but they might not know the lady from her men, nor one knight from another.

"Ah," said the King, "here may ye see the vengeance of God, and now I am sorry that this misadventure is befallen."

And then he looked for the scabbard, but it could not be found, so he returned to the abbey where he came from. When Arthur was gone, Queen Morgan turned all into the likeness as she and they were before, and said, "Sirs, now may we go where we will."

So she departed into the country of Gore, and there was she richly received, and made her castles and towns passing strong, for always she feared much King Arthur.

When the King had well rested him at the abbey, he rode unto Camelot, and found his Queen and his barons right glad of his coming. And when they heard of his strange adventures as is afore rehearsed, they all had marvel of the falsehood of Morgan le Fay, and many knights wished her burned because of her wicked enchantments. "Well," said the King, "I shall so be avenged on her, if I live, that all Christendom shall speak of it."

On the morn there came a damsel from Morgan to the King, and she brought with her the richest mantle that ever was seen in that court, for it was set as full of precious stones as one might stand by another, and there were the richest stones that ever the King saw. And the damsel said, "Your sister sendeth you this mantle, and desireth that ye should take this gift of her, and in what thing she hath offended you, she will amend it at your own pleasure."

When the King beheld this mantle it pleased him much, but he said little. With that came one of the Damsels of the Lake unto the King and said, "Sir, I must speak with you in private."

"Say on," said the King, "what ye will."

"Sir," said the damsel, "put not on you this mantle till ye have seen more, and in no wise let it come on you or any knight of yours, till ye command the bringer thereof to put it upon her."

"Well," said King Arthur, "it shall be done as ye counsel me." And then he said unto the damsel that came from his sister, "Damsel, this mantle that ye have brought me I will see upon you."

"Sir," said she, "it will not beseem me to wear a king's garment."

"By my head," said Arthur, "ye shall wear it ere it come on my back, or any man's that here is."

And so the King made it to be put upon her, and forthwithal she fell down dead, and nevermore spake word after, but burned to coals.

Then was the King wonderfully wroth, more than he was beforehand, and said unto King Uriens, "My sister, your wife, is alway about to betray me, and well I wot either ye or your son Sir Uwaine is of counsel with her to have me destroyed; but as for you," said the King to King Uriens, "I deem not greatly that ye be of her counsel, for she plotted with Accolon to destroy you as well as me. Therefore I hold you excused; but as for your son, Sir Uwaine, I hold him suspected, and therefore I charge you put him out of my court."

So Sir Uwaine was discharged. And when Sir Gawaine wist that, he made himself ready to go with his cousin. So they two departed, and rode into a great forest, and came to an abbey of monks, where they were well lodged. But when the King wist that Sir Gawaine was departed from the court, there was made great sorrow among all the estates.

"Now," said Gaheris, Gawaine's brother, "we have lost two good knights for the sake of one."

Sir Launcelot of the Lake

When King Arthur, after long wars, rested and held a royal feast with his allies and noble knights of the Round Table, there came into his hall, he sitting on his throne royal, twelve ambassadors from Rome, and said to him: "The high and mighty emperor Lucius sendeth to the king of Britain greeting, commanding thee to acknowledge him for thy lord and to send the tribute due from this realm unto the empire according to the statutes and decrees made by the noble and worthy Julius Caesar, conqueror of this realm and first emperor of Rome. And if thou refuse his demand and commandment, know thou for certain that he shall make strong war against thee, thy realms and lands, and shall chastise thee and thy subjects, so that it shall be warning perpetual unto all kings and princes not to deny their tribute unto the noble empire which dominateth the universal world."

Some of the young knights hearing this message would have run on the ambassadors to slay them, saying that it was a rebuke unto all the knights there present to suffer them to say so to the King. But King Arthur commanded that none should do them any harm, and anon let call all his lords and knights of the Round Table to council upon the matter. And all agreed to make sharp war on the Romans, and to aid after their power.

So the messengers were allowed to depart, and they took ship at Sandwich and passed forth by Flanders, Almaine, the mountains and all Italy until they came unto Rome. There they said to Lucius, "Certainly he is a lord to be feared, for his estate is the royalest that ever we saw, and in his person he is the most manly man that liveth, and is likely to conquer all the world, for unto his courage it is too little; wherefore we advise you to keep well your marches and straits[1] in the mountains."

Then Lucius made ready a great host and marched into Gaul, and Arthur met him there with his army. The old chronicles tell of the great battles that were fought and the brave deeds of knights and lords, how Arthur himself with Excalibur cleft the head of Lucius, and at length passed over the mountains into Lombardy and Tuscany, and so came into Rome. On a day appointed, as the romance telleth, he was crowned emperor by the Pope's hand with all the royalty that could be made.

After he had established all his lands from Rome unto France, and had given lands and realms unto his servants and knights, to each after his desert in such wise that none complained, rich nor poor, all his lords and all the great men of estate assembled before him and said: "Blessed be God, your war is finished and your conquest achieved, insomuch that we know none so great nor mighty that dare make war against you; wherefore we beseech you to return homeward and give us licence to go home to our wives, from whom we have been long, and to rest us, for your journey is finished with honour."

So they all came over sea, and landed at Sandwich, where Queen Guenever came and met the King. And he was nobly received of all the commons in every city and borough, and great gifts were presented to him at his home-coming, to welcome him.

Of all the knights that, when Arthur came into England, had increased in honour, Sir Launcelot of the Lake in especial excelled in deeds of arms both for life and death. His parents, King Ban of Benwick and his fair queen, Elaine, had first named him Galahad, and, as has already been said, Merlin, before he disappeared under the stone, had foretold that within twenty years he should be known over the whole world as a great and worthy knight. It is no marvel, therefore, that Launcelot is the first knight that the French book maketh mention of after King Arthur came from Rome. He passed with Arthur into England, where he was received gladly and was made a knight of the Round Table. Queen Guenever had him in great favour above all other knights, and in return he was loyal to her above all other ladies and damsels all his life, and for love of her he did many deeds of arms, and saved her from the fire through his noble chivalry. Therefore jealous people spoke evil of Sir Launcelot and the Queen, because they were of less prowess and honour than he, and thereby great mischief arose in Arthur's court. From this came Arthur's overthrow in the end, and the downfall of his noble realm.

But for long years Launcelot was the glory of knighthood, and he vied with King Arthur himself in deeds of prowess and of chivalrous courtesy in the tournament and on adventure.

[1] Strait: narrow pass.

A Night-Time Adventure of Sir Launcelot

In fulfilment of his oath as a knight of the Round Table Sir Launcelot rode into many strange and wild countries and through many waters and valleys. He slew Sir Turquine, who watched to destroy knights, and he clove the head of another false traitor who attended to destroy and distress ladies, damsels, and gentlewomen. Other wrongs besides these he righted, and bravely withstood many a struggle.

Now on a day it chanced that he passed a deep forest, where, as often before, he found strait lodging. But he was brave and strong, and feared no hardship provided he did nothing contrary to his honour as a worthy knight. As he was riding over a long bridge there started upon him suddenly a passing foul churl, who struck his horse upon the nose and asked Sir Launcelot why he rode over that bridge without licence.

"Why should I not ride this way?" said Sir Launcelot; "it is the way I choose to ride."

"Thou shall not choose," said the churl, and began to beat him with his great club shod with iron.

Sir Launcelot drew his sword, and made short work of this rough porter. Then he rode right on to the end of the bridge, through the fair village, where all the people in vain gave him warning, and on straight into the green courtyard of the castle, which was Tintagil, in Cornwall.

Anon there came upon him two great giants, with horrible clubs in their hands. With shield and sword he soon laid on the earth one of these giants. The other ran away for fear of the horrible strokes, and Sir Launcelot entered the hall. Here he set free three-score gentlewomen, who for seven years had been prisoners of the two giants, working all manner of silk works for their food.

"Show me such cheer as ye have," said Sir Launcelot, "and what treasure there is in this castle I give you for a reward for your grievance." Then soon he mounted his horse again, and rode away upon further adventure.

One night he came to the courtyard of an old gentleman, who lodged him with a good will, and there he had good cheer for himself and his horse. When time was his host brought him into a fair garret over the gate to his bed. There Sir Launcelot unarmed him, set his armour beside him, and went to bed, and anon fell asleep. Soon afterward there came one on horseback, and knocked at the gate in great haste. When Sir Launcelot heard this, he arose up and looked out at the window, and saw by the moonlight three knights come after that one man; all three lashed on him at once with swords, and that one knight turned on them knightly again and defended himself.

"Truly," said Sir Launcelot, "yonder one knight shall I help, for it were shame for me to see three knights on one, and if he be slain I am partner in his death."

Therewith he took his armour and let himself down from the window by a sheet to the four knights.

"Turn you knights unto me," cried Sir Launcelot aloud, "and leave your fighting with that knight."

And then they all three left Sir Kay, for it was he who was so hard bestead, and turned unto Sir Launcelot. And there began great battle, for they alighted, all three, and struck many great strokes at Sir Launcelot, and assailed him on every side. Sir Kay would have helped him, but Sir Launcelot suffered him not, and anon within six strokes he had struck all three to the earth. Sir Launcelot made them yield themselves to Sir Kay and promise to go next Whitsunday to the court as prisoners of Queen Guenever. So they were suffered to depart, and Sir Launcelot knocked at the gate with the pommel of his sword. The host came, and they entered, Sir Kay and he. "Sir," said the host, "I thought you were in your bed." "So I was," said Sir Launcelot, "but I arose and leaped out at my window to help an old fellow of mine."

When they came nigh the light, Sir Kay knew well that it was Sir Launcelot, and therewith he kneeled down and thanked him for all his kindness that he had holpen him from death.

"Sir," said Sir Launcelot, "I have done nothing but that I ought to do, and ye are welcome, and here shall ye repose you and take your rest."

So when Sir Kay was unarmed he asked for meat; there was meat fetched him, and he ate strongly. Then they went to their beds, and Sir Launcelot and Sir Kay were lodged together in one bed. On the morn Sir Launcelot arose early, and left Sir Kay sleeping. He put on Sir Kay's armour and took his shield, and so went to the stable. He here got Sir Kay's horse, took leave of his host, and so departed.

Then soon afterward Sir Kay arose. He missed Sir Launcelot, and then he espied that his armour and his horse had been taken. "Now by my faith," said he, "I know well that he will grieve some of the court of King Arthur, for my armour and horse will beguile all knights; they will believe it is I, and will be bold to him. And because I have his armour and shield I am sure I shall ride in peace." Then soon afterward Sir Kay thanked his host and departed.

So Sir Launcelot rode into a deep forest, and there in a dell he saw four knights standing under an oak, and they were of Arthur's court. Anon as they espied Sir Launcelot they thought by his arms it was Sir Kay.

"Now by my faith," said Sir Sagramour, one of the four knights, "I will prove Sir Kay's might"; so he got his spear in his hand, and came toward Sir Launcelot. Therewith Sir Launcelot was ware, and knew him well; and he smote Sir Sagramour so sore that horse and man fell both to the earth.

"Lo, my fellows," said Sir Ector, another of the four, "yonder ye may see what a buffet he hath; that knight is much bigger than ever was Sir Kay. Now shall ye see what I may do to him."

So Sir Ector got his spear in his hand and galloped toward Sir Launcelot, and Sir Launcelot smote him through shield and shoulder so that horse and man went to the earth, and ever his spear held.

"By my faith," said Sir Uwaine, "yonder is a strong knight, and I am sure he hath slain Sir Kay; and I see by his great strength it will be hard to match him."

Therewithal Sir Uwaine gat his spear in his hand and rode toward Sir Launcelot. Sir Launcelot knew him well, and so he met him on the plain, and gave him such a buffet that he was stunned, and long he wist not where he was.

"Now see I well," said Sir Gawaine, the last of the four knights, "I must encounter with that knight."

Then he dressed his shield and gat a good spear in his hand, and then they let run their horses with all their mights, and either knight smote other in midst of the shield. But Sir Gawaine's spear brake, and Sir Launcelot charged so sore upon him that his horse reversed up-so-down.

Much sorrow had Sir Gawaine to get clear of his horse, and so Sir Launcelot passed on a pace, and smiled, and said, "God give him joy that made this spear, for there came never a better in my hand."

Then the four knights went each one to other and comforted each other. "What say ye to this deed?" said Sir Gawaine. "He is a man of great might, for that one spear hath felled us four. I dare lay my head it is Sir Launcelot; I know it by his riding."

How Sir Launcelot Came into the Chapel Perilous

On a day as Sir Launcelot rode a great while in a deep forest, he was ware of an old manor beyond a bridge. And he passed over the bridge, that was old and feeble, and came into a great hall, where he saw lie a dead knight, that was a seemly man. And therewithal came out a lady weeping and wringing her hands, and she said: "Oh, knight, too much sorrow hast thou brought me."

"Why say ye so?" said Sir Launcelot; "I did never this knight any harm; therefore, fair lady, be not displeased with me, for I am full sore aggrieved at your grievance."

"Truly sir," she said, "I know it is not ye that have slain my husband, for he that did that deed is sore wounded, and he is never likely to recover; that I assure you."

"What was your husband's name?" asked Sir Launcelot.

"Sir," said she, "his name was Sir Gilbert, one of the best knights of the world, and he that hath slain him, I know not his name."

"God send you better comfort," said Sir Launcelot, and so he departed and went into the forest again, and there he met with a damsel who knew him well, and said aloud, "Well are ye come, my lord; and now I require thee on thy knighthood help my brother that is sore wounded, and never ceaseth bleeding, for this day fought he with Sir Gilbert and slew him in plain battle. My brother was sore wounded, and a sorceress that dwelleth in a castle hard by told me this day that my brother's wounds should never be whole till I could find a knight that would go into the Chapel Perilous where he should find a sword and a bloody cloth that the wounded knight was wrapped in. A piece of that cloth and the sword should heal my brother's wounds, if his wounds were searched with the sword and the cloth."

"This is a marvellous thing," said Sir Launcelot, "but what is your brother's name?"

"Sir," said she, "his name is Sir Meliot."

"That me repenteth," said Sir Launcelot, "for he is a fellow of the Table Round, and to help him I will do all in my power."

"Then, sir," said she, "follow this highway, and it will bring you into the Chapel Perilous, and here I shall wait till God send you again; except you I know no knight living that may achieve that adventure."

So Launcelot departed, and when he came unto the Chapel Perilous, he alighted and tied his horse to the little gate of the churchyard. And soon he saw on the front of the chapel many fair rich shields turned up-so-down, and many of these shields he had seen borne by knights that he had known aforetime. Then he saw standing there by him thirty great knights, taller by a yard than any man that ever he had seen, all clad in black armour, ready with their shields, and their swords drawn. They all grinned and gnashed at Sir Launcelot, and when he saw their countenances, he put his shield afore him, and took his sword in his hand ready unto battle. He started to go right past the giants, and then they scattered on every side and gave him the way. Therewith he waxed all bold and entered into the chapel, where he saw no light but a dim lamp burning, and soon became aware of a corpse covered with a cloth of silk. Sir Launcelot stooped down and cut off a piece of that cloth, whereupon the earth under him seemed to quake a little, and at this he feared. Then he saw a fair sword lying by the dead knight. This he gat into his hand and hied out of the chapel.

As soon as ever he was in the chapel yard all the giants spake to him with a grimly voice, and said: "Knight, Sir Launcelot, lay that sword from thee, or else thou shalt die."

"Whether I live or die," said Sir Launcelot, "no loud words will get it again; therefore fight for it if ye will."

Then he immediately passed right through their midst, and beyond the chapel yard there met him a fair damsel, who said, "Sir Launcelot, leave that sword behind thee, or thou wilt die for it."

"I leave it not," said Sir Launcelot, "for any entreaties."

"It is well," said she. "If thou didst leave that sword thou shouldst never see Queen Guenever again. Now, gentle knight, I request one thing of thee. Kiss me but once."

"Nay," said Sir Launcelot, "God forbid that I should do that."

"It is well, sir," said she; "if thou hadst kissed me thy life days had been done. But now, alas, I have lost all my labour, for I ordained this chapel to win thee. Once I had Sir Gawaine well nigh within my power, but he fought with that knight that lieth there dead in yonder chapel, Sir Gilbert, and smote off his left hand and so escaped. Sir Launcelot, I have loved thee these seven years, but now I know no woman may have thy love but Queen Guenever."

"Ye say well," said Sir Launcelot. "God preserve me from your subtile crafts."

Thereupon he took his horse and so departed from her, and soon met the damsel, Sir Meliot's sister. Anon she led him to the castle where Sir Meliot lay, pale as the earth from bleeding. Sir Launcelot leaped unto him and touched his wounds with Sir Gilbert's sword, and then wiped his wounds with a part of the cloth that Sir Gilbert was wrapped in, and anon he was as whole a man as ever he had been in all his life. And then there was great joy between them. They made Sir Launcelot all the cheer that they might, and on the morn he took his leave of Sir Meliot and his sister, and rode away.

The Knight, the Lady, and the Falcon

And Sir Launcelot by fortune came to a fair castle, and as he passed by he was ware of a falcon that came flying over his head toward a high elm. As the bird flew into the tree to take her perch, the long lines about her feet caught on a bough, and when she would take flight again she hung fast by the legs. Sir Launcelot saw how the fair falcon hung there, and he was sorry for her.

Meanwhile came a lady out of the castle and cried aloud, "O Launcelot, Launcelot, as thou art the flower of all knights, help me to get my hawk. I was holding my hawk and she slipped from me, and if my lord my husband knows that she is lost he will slay me."

"What is your lord's name?" said Sir Launcelot.

"Sir," said the lady, "his name is Sir Phelot, a knight of Northgalis."

"Well, fair lady," said Launcelot, "since ye know my name, and request me as a courteous knight to help you, I will do what I may to get your hawk. And yet truly I am an ill climber, and the tree is passing high, with few boughs to cling to."

Thereupon Sir Launcelot alighted, and tied his horse to the elm. Then the lady helped him to unarm, and with might and force he climbed up to the falcon. He tied the lines to a great rotten branch, brake it off, and threw it and the hawk down. Anon the lady gat the hawk in her hand, and thereupon came Sir Phelot suddenly out of the grove, all armed and with his naked sword in his hand. He called up to Sir Launcelot and said, "O knight, now have I found thee as I would"; and he stood at the foot of the tree to slay him.

"Ah lady," said Sir Launcelot, "why have ye betrayed me?"

"She hath done," said Sir Phelot, "but as I commanded her; there is no help for it; thine hour is come, and thou must die."

"It were shame unto thee," said Sir Launcelot, "for thee, an armed knight, to slay an unarmed man by treason."

"Thou gettest no other grace," said Sir Phelot; "therefore help thyself if thou canst."

"Alas," said Sir Launcelot, "that ever knight should die weaponless."

Then he looked above and below him, and saw a big leafless bough. This he brake off; then he climbed down with it in his hand, and, observing how his horse stood, he suddenly leaped down to the ground on the farther side of the horse from the knight.

Then Sir Phelot lashed at him eagerly, thinking to slay him. But Sir Launcelot put away the stroke with the branch, and then with it gave Sir Phelot such a blow on one side of the head that he fell down in a swoon to the ground. Then Sir Launcelot took his sword out of his hand and struck his head from his body.

"Alas," cried the lady, "why hast thou slain my husband?"

"I am not the cause," said Sir Launcelot, "for with falsehood ye would have slain me by treason, and now it is fallen on you both."

Thereupon Sir Launcelot gat all his armour as well as he might, and put it on for fear of further attack, since the knight's castle was so near. As soon as he might he took his horse, and, thanking God that he had escaped that adventure, he went on his adventures over many wild ways, through marsh and valley and forest.

At Pentecost he returned home, and the King and all the court were passing glad of his coming. And ever now and now came all the knights back, those that had encountered with Sir Launcelot, those that he had set free from prison, and all those that knew of his great deeds of arms. And they all bare record of Sir Launcelot's prowess, so at that time he had the greatest name of any knight of the world, and most he was honoured of high and low.

How a Kitchen-Page Came to Honour

Arthur was holding the high feast of Pentecost at a city and castle called in those days Kink-Kenadon, upon the sands nigh Wales, and he sat at meat with all the knights of the Round Table. Then came into the hall two men well beseen and richly, and upon their shoulders there leaned the goodliest young man and the fairest that ever any of the knights had seen. He was higher than the other two by a foot and a half, broad in the shoulders, well visaged, and the fairest and largest handed that ever man saw; but he acted as though he might not walk nor support himself unless he leaned upon their shoulders. They went with him right unto the high dais without saying of any words.

Then this much young man pulled himself away, and easily stretched up straight, saying: "King Arthur, God you bless and all your fair fellowship of the Round Table. For this cause I am come hither, to pray you to give me three gifts. They shall not be so unreasonable but that ye may honourably grant them me, and to you no great hurt nor loss. The first I will ask now, and the other two gifts I will ask this day twelvemonth wheresoever ye hold your high feast."

"Now ask," said Arthur, "and ye shall have your asking."

"Now, sir, this is my petition for this feast, that you will give me meat and drink sufficiently for this twelve-month, and at that day I will ask mine other two gifts."

"This is but a simple asking," said the King; "ye shall have meat and drink enough; I never refuse that to any, neither my friend nor my foe. But what is your name I would know?"

"I cannot tell you," said he.

The King marvelled at this answer, but took him to Sir Kay, the steward, and charged him that he should give the youth of all manner of meats and drinks of the best, and also that he should have all manner of finding as though he were a lord's son.

"That need not be," said Sir Kay, "to do such cost upon him; for I dare undertake he is a villain born, and never will make a man, for had he come of gentlemen he would have asked of you horse and armour; but such as he is, so he asketh. And since he hath no name, I shall give him the name

Beaumains, that is Fair-hands, and into the kitchen I shall bring him, and there he shall have rich broth every day, so that he shall be as fat by the twelvemonth's end as a pork hog."

So the two men departed, and left him to Sir Kay, who scorned him and mocked him. Thereat was Sir Gawaine wroth, and especially Sir Launcelot bade Sir Kay leave off his mocking, "for," said he, "I dare wager he shall prove a man of great honour."

"It may not be by any reason," said Sir Kay, "for as he is, so hath he asked."

So Sir Kay ordered that a place be made for him, and Fair-hands went to the hall door, and sat down among boys and lads, and there he ate sadly. After meat Sir Launcelot bade him come to his chamber, where he should have meat and drink enough, and so did Sir Gawaine; but he refused them all; he would do none other but as Sir Kay commanded him. As touching Sir Gawaine, he had reason to proffer him lodging, meat, and drink, for he was nearer kin to him than he knew. But what Sir Launcelot did was of his great gentleness and courtesy.

Thus Fair-hands was put into the kitchen, and lay nightly as the boys of the kitchen did. And so he endured all that twelvemonth, and never displeased man nor child, but always he was meek and mild. But ever when there was any jousting of knights, that would he see if he could. And where were any masteries done, thereat would he be, and there might none cast bar nor stone to him by two yards. Then would Sir Kay say, "How like you my boy of the kitchen?"

So it passed on till the least of Whitsuntide, which at that time the King held at Carlion in the most royal wise that might be, as he did every year. As he again sat at meat, there came a damsel into the hall and saluted the King, and prayed him for succour. "For whom?" said the King; "what is the adventure?"

"Sir," she said, "I have a lady of great honour and renown, and she is besieged by a tyrant so that she may not out of her castle. And because your knights are called the noblest of the world, I come to you to pray you for succour."

"What is the name of your lady? and where dwelleth she? and who is he, and what is his name, that hath besieged her?"

"Sir King," she said, "as for my lady's name, that shall not ye know from me at this time, but I let you know she is a lady of great honour and of great lands. And as for the tyrant that besiegeth and destroyeth her lands, he is called the Red Knight of the Red Lawns."

"I know him not," said the King.

"Sir," said Sir Gawaine, "I know him well, for he is one of the most dangerous knights of the world. Men say that he hath seven men's strength, and from him I escaped once full hard with my life."

"Fair damsel," said the King, "there be knights here would do their best to rescue your lady, but because ye will not tell her name, nor where she dwelleth, therefore none of my knights that be here now shall go with you by my will."

"Then must I speak further," said the damsel.

With these words Fair-hands came before the King, while the damsel was there, and thus he said: "Sir King, God reward you, I have been these twelve months in your kitchen, and have had my full sustenance, and now I will ask my two gifts that be behind."

"Ask upon my peril," said the King.

"Sir, these shall be my two gifts. First, that ye will grant me this adventure of the damsel, and second, that ye shall bid Launcelot of the Lake to make me knight, for of him I will be made knight, and else of none. I pray you let him ride after me, and make me knight when I request him."

"All this shall be done," said the King.

"Fie on thee," said the damsel, "shall I have none but one that is your kitchen-page?" Then was she wroth, and took her horse and departed.

Thereupon there came one to Fair-hands, and told him that his horse and armour was come for him, with all things that he needed in the richest manner. Thereat all the court had much marvel from whence came all that gear. When he was armed and came into the hall to take leave of King Arthur and Sir Gawaine and Sir Launcelot, there were but few so goodly knights as he was. He prayed Sir Launcelot that he would hie after him, and so departed and rode after the damsel.

Many people followed after Fair-hands to behold how well he was horsed and trapped in cloth of gold, but he had neither shield nor spear. Then Sir

Kay said all openly in the hall, "I will ride after my boy of the kitchen, to see whether he will know me for his better."

Sir Launcelot and Sir Gawaine counselled him to abide at home; nevertheless he made ready and took his horse and his spear and rode off. Just as Fair-hands overtook the damsel, Sir Kay came up, and said, "Fair-hands, what sir, know ye not me?"

Then he turned his horse, and knew it was Sir Kay, that had done him all the despite, as we have heard afore. "Yea," said Fair-hands, "I know you for an ungentle knight of the court and therefore beware of me."

Therewith Sir Kay put his spear in its rest, and ran straight upon him, and Fair-hands came on just as fast with his sword in his hand. And so he put away his spear with his sword, and with a foin[1] thrust him through the side, so that Sir Kay fell down as if he were dead. Then Fair-hands alighted down and took Sir Kay's shield and his spear, had his dwarf mount upon Sir Kay's horse, and started upon his own horse and rode his way. All this Sir Launcelot saw, and so did the damsel.

By this time Sir Launcelot had come up, and Fair-hands offered to joust with him. So they rushed together like boars, and for upwards of an hour they had a hard fight, wherein Sir Launcelot had so much ado with Fair-hands that he feared himself to be shamed. At length he said, "Fair-hands, fight not so sore; your quarrel and mine is not so great but we may leave off."

"That is truth," said Fair-hands, "but it doth me good to feel your might, and yet, my lord, I showed not my uttermost."

"Well," said Sir Launcelot, "I promise you I had as much to do as I might to save myself from you unashamed; therefore ye need have no fear of any earthly knight."

"Hope ye then," said Fair-hands, "that I may anywhere stand as a proved knight?"

"Yea," said Launcelot, "do as ye have done, and I shall be your warrant."

"Then I pray you give me the order of knighthood," said Fair-hands.

"Then must ye tell me your name," said Launcelot, "and of what kin ye be born."

"Sir, if ye will not make me known, I will," said Fair-hands.

"That I promise you by the faith of my body, until it be openly known," said Sir Launcelot.

"Then, sir," he said, "my name is Gareth; I am own brother unto Sir Gawaine."

"Ah! sir," said Launcelot, "I am more glad of you than I was, for ever me thought ye should be of great blood, and that ye came not to the court either for meat or for drink."

Then Sir Launcelot gave him the order of knighthood, and Sir Gareth went his way.

Sir Launcelot now came to Sir Kay and had him carried home upon his shield. He was with difficulty healed of his wounds, and all men scorned him. In especial Sir Gawaine and Sir Launcelot said it was not for Sir Kay to rebuke the young man, for full little he knew of what birth he was and for what cause he came to this court.

[1] Foin: reach forth.

How Sir Gareth Fought for the Lady of Castle Perilous

After the damsel rode Fair-hands, now well provided with shield and spear, and known to Sir Launcelot, at least, as Sir Gareth and nephew to King Arthur. When he had overtaken the damsel, anon she said: "What dost thou here? Thou smellest all of the kitchen; thy clothes be foul with the grease and tallow that thou gainedst in King Arthur's kitchen; therefore turn again, foul kitchen-page. I know thee well, for Sir Kay named thee Fair-hands. What art thou but a lubber and a turner of spits, and a ladle washer?"

"Damsel," said Fair-hands, "say to me what ye will, I will not go from you, for I have undertaken, in King Arthur's presence, to achieve your adventure, and so shall I finish it, or I shall die therefore."

Thus as they rode along in the wood, there came a man flying all that ever he might. "Whither wilt thou?" said Fair-hands.

"O lord," he said, "help me, for yonder in a dell are six thieves that have taken my lord and bound him, and I am afeard lest they will slay him."

So Fair-hands rode with the man until they came to where the knight lay bound, and the thieves hard by. Fair-hands struck one unto the death, and then another, and at the third stroke he slew the third thief; and then the other three fled. He rode after them and overtook them, and then those three thieves turned again and assailed Fair-hands hard, but at the last he slew them also, and returned and unbound the knight. The knight thanked him, and prayed him to ride with him to his castle there a little beside, and he should honourably reward him for his good deeds.

"Sir," said Fair-hands, "I will no reward have except as God reward me. And also I must follow this damsel."

When he came nigh her, she bade him ride from her, "for," said she, "thou smellest all of the kitchen; thinkest thou that I have joy of thee? All this deed thou hast done is but mishapped thee, but thou shalt see a sight that shall make thee turn again, and that lightly."

Then the same knight who was rescued from the thieves rode after that damsel, and prayed her to lodge with him that night. And because it was near night the damsel rode with him to the castle, and there they had great cheer. At supper the knight set Sir Fair-hands afore the damsel.

"Fie, fie," said she, "sir knight, ye are uncourteous to set a kitchen-page afore me; him beseemeth better to stick a swine than to sit afore a damsel of high parentage."

Then the knight was ashamed at her words, and took Fair-hands up and set him at a sideboard, and seated himself afore him. So all that night they had good cheer and merry rest.

On the morn the damsel and Fair-hands thanked the knight and took their leave, and rode on their way until they came to a great forest. Therein was a great river with but one passage, and there were ready two knights on the farther side, to prevent their crossing. Fair-hands would not have turned back had there been six more, and he rushed into the water. One of the two encountered with him in the midst of the stream, and both spears were broken. Then they drew their swords and smote eagerly at one another. At the last Sir Fair-hands smote the other upon the helm so that he fell down stunned in the water, and there was he drowned. Then Sir Fair-hands spurred his horse upon the land, where the other fell upon him, and they fought long together. At the last Sir Fair-hands clove his helm and his head, and so rode unto the damsel and bade her ride forth on her way.

"Alas," she said, "that ever a kitchen-page should have that fortune to destroy two such doughty knights. Thou thinkest thou hast done doughtily, but that is not so, for the first knight's horse stumbled, and so he was drowned in the water; it was never by thy force or by thy might. And as for the second knight, by mishap thou camest behind him and slewest him."

"Damsel," said Fair-hands, "ye may say what ye will, but whomsoever I have ado with I trust to God to serve him ere he depart, and therefore I reck not what ye say, provided I may win your lady."

"Fie, fie, foul kitchen-knave, thou shalt see knights that shall abate thy boast. I see all that ever thou doest is but by misadventure, and not by prowess of thy hands."

"Fair damsel," said he, "give me goodly language, and then my care is past. Ye may say what ye will; what knights soever I shall meet, I fear them not, and wheresoever ye go I will follow you."

So they rode on till even-song time, and ever she chid him and would not cease. And then they came to a black lawn, and there was a black hawthorn, and thereon hung a black banner, and on the other side there hung a black shield, and by it stood a black spear great and long, and a great black horse covered with silk, and a black stone fast by, whereon sat a knight all armed in black harness, and his name was the Knight of the Black Lawns.

The damsel, when she saw this knight, bade Fair-hands flee down the valley. "Grammercy," said he, "always ye would have me a coward."

With that the Black Knight, when she came nigh him, spake and said, "Damsel, have ye brought this knight of King Arthur to be your champion?"

"Nay, fair knight," said she, "this is but a kitchen-knave, that was fed in King Arthur's kitchen for alms. I cannot be rid of him, for with me he rideth against my will. Would that ye should put him from me, or else slay him, if ye may, for he is a troublesome knave, and evilly he hath done this day."

"Thus much shall I grant you," said the Black Knight: "I shall put him down upon one foot, and his horse and his harness he shall leave with me, for it were shame to me to do him any more harm."

When Sir Fair-hands heard him say thus, he said, "Sir knight, thou art full generous with my horse and my harness; I let thee know it cost thee naught, and whether thou like it or not, this lawn will I pass, and neither horse nor harness gettest thou of me, except as thou win them with thy hands. I am no kitchen-page, as the damsel saith I am; I am a gentleman born, and of more high lineage than thou, and that will I prove on thy body."

Then in great wrath they drew back with their horses, and rushed together as it had been the thunder. The Black Knight's spear brake, and Fair-hands thrust him through both his sides, whereupon his own spear brake also. Nevertheless the Black Knight drew his sword and smote many eager strokes of great might, and hurt Fair-hands full sore. But at the last he fell down off his horse in a swoon, and there he died.

When Fair-hands saw that the Black Knight had been so well horsed and armed, he alighted down and armed himself in the dead man's armour, took his horse, and rode after the damsel. When she saw him come nigh, she said, "Away, kitchen-knave, out of the wind, for the smell of thy foul clothes offendeth me. Alas that ever such a knave as thou art should by mishap slay so good a knight as thou hast done. All this is my ill luck, but hard by is one that shall requite thee, and therefore again I counsel thee, flee."

"It may be my lot," said Fair-hands, "to be beaten or slain, but I warn you, fair damsel, I will not flee away or leave your company for all that ye can say, for ever ye say that they will kill me or beat me, yet it happeneth that I escape and they lie on the ground. Therefore it were as good for you to stop thus all day rebuking me, for away will I not till I see the uttermost of this journey, or else I will be slain or truly beaten; therefore ride on your way, for follow you I will, whatsoever happen."

As they rode along together they saw a knight come driving by them all in green, both his horse and his harness; and when he came nigh the damsel he asked her, "Is that my brother the Black Knight that ye have brought with you?"

"Nay, nay," said she, "this unlucky kitchen-knave hath slain your brother through mischance."

"Alas," said the Green Knight, "that is great pity that so noble a knight as he was should so unfortunately be slain, and by a knave's hand, as ye say that he is. Ah! traitor, thou shalt die for slaying my brother; he was a full noble knight."

"I defy thee," said Fair-hands, "for I make known to thee I slew him knightly and not shamefully."

Therewithal the Green Knight rode unto a horn that was green that hung on a green thorn, and there he blew three deadly notes, whereupon came two damsels and armed him lightly. Then he took a great horse and a green shield and a green spear, and the two knights ran together with all their mights. They brake their spears unto their hands, and then drew their swords. Now they gave many sad strokes, and either of them wounded other full ill.

At the last Fair-hands' horse struck the Green Knight's horse upon the side, and it fell to the earth. Then the Green Knight left his horse lightly, and prepared to fight on foot. That saw Fair-hands, and therewithal he alighted, and they rushed together like two mighty champions a long while, and sore they bled both.

With that came the damsel and said, "My lord, the Green Knight, why for shame stand ye so long fighting with the kitchen-knave? Alas, it is shame that ever ye were made knight, to see such a lad match such a knight, as if the weed overgrew the corn."

Therewith the Green Knight was ashamed, and gave a great stroke of might, and clave Fair-hands' shield through. When the young knight saw his shield cloven asunder he was a little ashamed of that stroke and of her language, and then he gave the other such a buffet upon the helm that he fell on his knees, and Fair-hands quickly pulled him upon the ground grovelling. Then the Green Knight cried for mercy, and yielded himself unto Sir Fair-hands, and prayed him to slay him not.

"All is in vain," said Fair-hands, "for thou shalt die unless this damsel that came with me pray me to save thy life."

Therewithal he unlaced his helm as if to slay him. "Let be," said the damsel, "thou foul kitchen-knave, slay him not, for if thou do, thou shalt repent it."

"Damsel," said Fair-hands, "your charge is to me a pleasure, and at your commandment his life shall be saved, and else not. Sir Knight with the green arms, I release thee quit at this damsel's request, for I will not make her wroth; I will fulfil all that she chargeth me."

And then the Green Knight kneeled down and did him homage with his sword, promising for ever to become his man together with thirty knights that held of him. Then said the damsel, "Me repenteth, Green Knight, of your damage and of the death of your brother the Black Knight; of your help I had great need, for I fear me sore to pass this forest."

"Nay, fear ye not," said the Green Knight, "for ye shall lodge with me this night, and to-morn I shall help you through this forest."

So they took their horses and rode to his manor, which was fast there beside. And ever the damsel rebuked Fair-hands, and would not suffer him to sit at her table. But the Green Knight took him and set him at a side table, and did him honour, for he saw that he was come of noble blood and had proved himself a full noble knight. All that night he commanded thirty men privily to watch Fair-hands for to keep him from all treason. And on the morn they arose, and after breaking their fast they took their horses and rode on their way.

As the Green Knight conveyed them through the forest he said, "My lord Fair-hands, I and these thirty knights shall be always at your summons, both early and late at your call wherever ye will send us."

"It is well," said Fair-hands; "when I call upon you ye must go unto King Arthur with all your knights."

So the Green Knight took his leave, and the damsel said unto Fair-hands, "Why followest thou me, thou kitchen-boy; cast away thy shield and thy spear and flee, for thou shalt not pass a pass here, that is called the pass Perilous."

"Damsel," said Fair-hands, "who is afraid let him flee, for it were shame to turn again since I have ridden so long with you."

"Well," said she, "ye shall soon, whether ye will or not."

In like manner on the next day Sir Fair-hands overcame a third brother, the Red Knight, and in like manner the damsel would have Fair-hands spare his life. Albeit she spake unto him many contemptuous words, whereof the Red Knight had great marvel, and all that night made three-score men to watch Fair-hands that he should have no shame or villainy. The Red Knight yielded himself to Fair-hands with fifty knights, and they all proffered him homage and fealty at all times to do him service.

"I thank you," said Fair-hands; "this ye shall grant me when I call upon you, to come afore my lord King Arthur and yield yourselves unto him to be his knights."

"Sir," said the Red Knight, "I will be ready and my fellowship at your summons."

So again upon the morn Sir Fair-hands and the damsel departed, and ever she rode chiding him in the foulest manner.

"Damsel," said Fair-hands, "ye are uncourteous so to rebuke me as ye do, for me seemeth I have done you good service, and ever ye threaten me I shall be beaten with knights that we meet; but ever for all your boasts they lie in the dust or in the mire, and therefore I pray you rebuke me no more. When ye see me beaten or yielded as recreant, then may ye bid me go from you shamefully, but first I let you wit I will not depart from you, for I were worse than a fool if I should depart from you all the while that I win honour."

"Well," said she, "right soon there shall come a knight that shall pay thee all thy wages, for he is the most man of honour of the world, except King Arthur."

"The more he is of honour," said Fair-hands, "the more shall be my honour to have ado with him. Have no doubt, damsel, by the grace of God

I shall so deal with this knight that within two hours after noon I shall overcome him, and then shall we come to the siege of your lady's castle seven miles hence by daylight."

"Marvel have I," said the damsel, "what manner of man ye be, for it may never be otherwise but that ye be come of noble blood, for so foul and shamefully did never woman rule a knight as I have done you, and ever courteously ye have suffered me, and that came never but of gentle blood."

"Damsel," said Fair-hands, "a knight may little do that may not suffer a damsel, for whatsoever ye said unto me I took no heed to your words, for the more ye said the more ye angered me, and my wrath I wreaked upon them that I had ado withal. And therefore all the missaying that ye missaid me furthered me in my battle, and caused me to think to show and prove myself at the end what I was. For peradventure, though I had meat in King Arthur's kitchen, yet I might have had meat enough in other places. All that I did to prove and to assay my friends, and whether I be a gentleman born or not, I let you wit, fair damsel, I have done you gentleman's service, and peradventure better service yet will I do ere I depart from you."

"Alas," she said, "good Fair-hands, forgive me all that I have missaid or done against thee."

"With all my heart," said he, "I forgive it you, and damsel, since it liketh you to say thus fair to me, wit ye well it gladdeth mine heart greatly, and now me seemeth there is no knight living but I am able enough for him."

With this Sir Persant of Inde, the fourth of the brethren that stood in Fair-hands' way to the siege, espied them as they came upon the fair meadow where his pavilion was. Sir Persant was the most lordly knight that ever thou lookedst on. His pavilion and all manner of thing that there is about, men and women, and horses' trappings, shields and spears were all of dark blue colour. Anon he and Fair-hands prepared themselves and rode against one another that both their spears were shattered to pieces, and their horses fell dead to the earth. Then they fought two hours and more on foot, until their armour was all hewn to pieces, and in many places they were wounded. At the last, though loath to do it, Fair-hands smote Sir Persant above upon the helm so that he fell grovelling to the earth, and the fierce battle was at an end. Like his three brethren before, Sir Persant yielded himself and asked for mercy, and at the damsel's request

Fair-hands gladly granted his life, and received homage and fealty from him and a hundred knights, to be always at his commandment.

On the morn as the damsel and Sir Fair-hands departed from Sir Persant's pavilion, "Fair damsel," said Persant, "whitherward are ye away leading this knight?"

"Sir," she said, "this knight is going to the siege that besiegeth my sister in the Castle Perilous."

"Ah, ah," said Persant, "that is the Knight of the Red Lawns, the most perilous knight that I know now living, a man that is without mercy, and men say that he hath seven men's strength. God save you, sir, from that knight, for he doth great wrong to that lady, which is great pity, for she is one of the fairest ladies of the world, and me seemeth that this damsel is her sister. Is not your name Linet?"

"Yea, sir," said she, "and my lady my sister's name is Dame Liones. Now, my lord Sir Persant of Inde, I request you that ye make this gentleman knight or ever he fight with the Red Knight."

"I will with all my heart," said Sir Persant, "if it please him to take the order of knighthood of so simple a man as I am."

But Fair-hands thanked him for his good will, and told him he was better sped, as the noble Sir Launcelot had already made him knight. Then, after Persant and the damsel had promised to keep it close, he told them his real name was Gareth of Orkney, King Arthur's nephew, and that Sir Gawaine and Sir Agravaine and Sir Gaheris were all his brethren, he being the youngest of them all. "And yet," said he, "wot not King Arthur nor Sir Gawaine what I am."

The book saith that the lady that was besieged had word of her sister's coming and a knight with her, and how he had passed all the perilous passages, had won all the four brethren, and had slain the Black Knight, and how he overthrew Sir Kay, and did great battle with Sir Launcelot, and was made knight by him. She was glad of these tidings, and sent them wine and dainty foods and bade Sir Fair-hands be of good heart and good courage.

The next day Fair-hands and Linet took their horses again and rode through a fair forest and came to a spot where they saw across the plain many pavilions and a fair castle and much smoke. And when they came near the siege Sir Fair-hands espied upon great trees, as he rode, how there hung goodly armed knights by the necks, nigh forty of them, their shields about their necks with their swords. These were knights that had come to the siege to rescue Dame Liones, and had been overcome and put to this shameful death by the Red Knight of the Red Lawns.

Then they rode to the dykes, and saw how strong were the defences, and many great lords nigh the walls, and the sea upon the one side of the walls, where were many ships and mariners' noise, with "hale" and "ho." Fast by there was a sycamore tree, whereupon hung a horn, the greatest that ever they saw, of an elephant's bone. This the Knight of the Red Lawns had hung up there that any errant knight might blow it, if he wished the Knight of the Red Lawns to come to him to do battle. The damsel Linet besought Fair-hands not to blow the horn till high noon, for the Red Knight's might grew greater all through the morn, till, as men said, he had seven men's strength.

"Ah, fie for shame, fair damsel," said Fair-hands, "say ye never so more to me, for, were he as good a knight as ever was, I shall never fail him in his most might, for either I will win honour honourably, or die knightly in the field."

Therewith he spurred his horse straight to the sycamore tree, and blew the horn so eagerly that all the siege and all the castle rang thereof. And then there leaped out knights out of their tents, and they within the castle looked over the walls and out at windows. Then the Red Knight of the Red Lawns armed himself hastily, and two barons set his spurs upon his heels, and all was blood red,—his armour, spear, and shield. And an earl buckled his helm upon his head, and then they brought him a red steed, and so he rode into a little vale under the castle, that all that were in the castle and at the siege might behold the battle.

Sir Fair-hands looked up at a window of the castle, and there he saw the Lady Liones, the fairest lady, it seemed to him, that ever he looked upon. She made courtesy down to him, and ever he looked up to the window with glad countenance, and loved her from that time and vowed to rescue her or else to die.

"Leave, Sir Knight, thy looking," said the Red Knight, "and behold me, I counsel thee, and make thee ready."

Then they both put their spears in their rests, and came together with all the might that they had. Either smote other in the midst of the shield with such force that the breastplates, horse-girths, and cruppers brake, and both fell to the earth stunned, and lay so long that all they that were in the castle and in the siege thought their necks had been broken. But at length they put their shields afore them, drew their swords, and ran together like two fierce lions. Either gave other such buffets upon the helm that they reeled backward; then they recovered both, and hewed off great pieces of their harness and their shields.

Thus they fought till it was past noon, and never would stint, till at last they lacked wind both, and stood panting and blowing a while. Then they went to battle again, and thus they endured till even-song time, and none that beheld them might know whether was like to win. Then by assent of them both they granted either other to rest; and so they sat down on two molehills, and unlaced their helms to take the cool wind. Then Sir Fair-hands looked up at the window, and there he saw the fair lady, Dame Liones. She made him such countenance that his heart waxed light and jolly; and therewith he bade the Red Knight of the Red Lawns make ready to do battle to the uttermost.

So they laced up their helms and fought freshly. By a cross stroke the Red Knight of the Red Lawns smote Sir Fair-hands' sword from him, and then gave him another buffet on the helm so that he fell grovelling to the earth, and the Red Knight fell upon him to hold him down. Then Linet cried to him aloud and said that the lady beheld and wept. When Sir Fair-hands heard her say so he started up with great might, gat upon his feet, and leaped to his sword. He gripped it in his hand, doubled his pace unto the Red Knight, and there they fought a new battle together.

Now Sir Fair-hands doubled his strokes and smote so thick that soon he had the better of the Red Knight of the Red Lawns, and unlaced his helm to slay him, whereupon he yielded himself to Fair-hands' mercy.

Sir Fair-hands bethought him upon the knights that he had made to be hanged shamefully, and said, "I may not with my honour save thy life."

Then came there many earls and barons and noble knights, and prayed Fair-hands to save his life and take him as prisoner. Then he released him upon this covenant that he go within to the castle and yield himself there to the lady, and if she would forgive him he might have his life with making amends to the lady of all the trespass he had done against her and her lands.

The Red Knight of the Red Lawns promised to do as Sir Fair-hands commanded and so with all those earls and barons he made his homage and fealty to him. Within a while he went unto the castle, where he made peace with the Lady Liones, and departed unto the court of King Arthur. There he told openly how he was overcome and by whom, and also he told all the battles of Fair-hands from the beginning unto the ending.

"Mercy," said King Arthur and Sir Gawaine, "we marvel much of what blood he is come, for he is a noble knight." But Sir Launcelot had no marvel, for he knew whence he came, yet because of his promise he would not discover Fair-hands until he permitted it or else it were known openly by some other.

Dame Liones soon learned through her brother Sir Gringamore that the knight who had wrought her deliverance was a king's son, Sir Gareth of Orkney, and nephew of King Arthur himself. And she made him passing good cheer, and he her again, and they had goodly language and lovely countenance together. And she promised the noble knight Sir Gareth certainly to love him and none other the days of her life. Then there was not a gladder man than he, for ever since he saw her at the window of Castle Perilous he had so burned in love for her that he was nigh past himself in his reason.

How Sir Gareth Returned to the Court of King Arthur

Now leave we Sir Gareth there with Sir Gringamore and his sisters, Liones and Linet, and turn we unto King Arthur that held the next feast of Pentecost at Carlion. And there came the Green Knight with his fifty knights, and they yielded themselves all unto King Arthur. And so there came the Red Knight, his brother, and yielded himself and three-score knights with him. Also there came the Blue Knight, brother to them, and his hundred knights, and yielded themselves. These three brethren told King Arthur how they were overcome by a knight that a damsel had with her, and called him Fair-hands. Also they told how the fourth brother, the Black Knight, was slain in an encounter with Sir Fair-hands, and of the adventure with the two brethren that kept the passage of the water; and ever more King Arthur marvelled who the knight might be that was in his kitchen a twelvemonth and that Sir Kay in scorn named Fair-hands.

Right as the King stood so talking with these three brethren there came Sir Launcelot of the Lake and told him that there was come a goodly lord with six hundred knights. The King went out, and there came to him and saluted him in a goodly manner the Red Knight of the Red Lawns, and he said, "I am sent to you by a knight that is called Fair-hands, for he won me in plain battle, hand for hand. No knight has ever had the better of me before. I and my knights yield ourselves to your will, as he commanded, to do you such service as may be in our power."

King Arthur received him courteously, as he had before received the three brethren, and he promised to do them honour for the love of Sir Fair-hands. Then the King and they went to meat, and were served in the best manner.

And as they sat at the table, there came in the Queen of Orkney, with ladies and knights a great number. And her sons, Sir Gawaine, Sir Agravaine, and Gaheris arose and went to her, and saluted her upon their knees and asked her blessing, for in fifteen years they had not seen her.

Then she spake on high to her brother, King Arthur, "Where have ye done my young son, Sir Gareth? He was here amongst you a twelvemonth, and ye made a kitchen-knave of him, which is shame to you all."

"Oh dear mother," said Sir Gawaine, "I knew him not."

"Nor I," said the King; "but thanked be God, he is proved an honourable knight as any of his years now living, and I shall never be glad till I may find him. Sister, me seemeth ye might have done me to know of his coming, and then, had I not done well to him, ye might have blamed me. For when he came to this court, he came leaning upon two men's shoulders, as though he might not walk. And then he asked of me three gifts,—one the same day, that was that I would give him meat for that twelvemonth. The other two gifts he asked that day a twelvemonth, and those were that he might have the adventure of the damsel Linet, and that Sir Launcelot should make him knight when he desired him. I granted him all his desire, and many in this court marvelled that he desired his sustenance for a twelvemonth, and thereby deemed many of us that he was not come of a noble house."

"Sir," said the Queen of Orkney unto King Arthur, her brother, "I sent him unto you right well armed and horsed, and gold and silver plenty to spend."

"It may be," said the King, "but thereof saw we none, save that same day as he departed from us, knights told me that there came a dwarf hither suddenly, and brought him armour and a good horse, full well and richly beseen, and thereat we had all marvel from whence that riches came. Then we deemed all that he was come of men of honour."

"Brother," said the queen, "all that ye say I believe, for ever since he was grown he was marvellously witted, and ever he was faithful and true to his promise. But I marvel that Sir Kay did mock him and scorn him, and give him the name Fair-hands. Yet Sir Kay named him more justly than he knew, for I dare say, if he be alive, he is as fair-handed a man and as well disposed as any living."

"Sister," said Arthur, "by the grace of God he shall be found if he be within these seven realms. Meanwhile let us be merry, for he is proved to be a man of honour, and that is my joy."

So then goodly letters were made and a messenger sent forth to the Lady Liones, praying her to give best counsel where Sir Gareth might be found. She answered that she could not then tell where he was; but she let proclaim a great tournament at her castle, and was sure that Sir Gareth would be heard of there. So King Arthur and all his knights of valour and prowess came together at the Lady Liones' castle by the Isle of Avilion, and great deeds of arms were done there, but most of all Sir Gareth gained honour, though no one knew that it was he until a herald rode near him and saw his name written about his helm.

Wit ye well the King made great joy when he found Sir Gareth again, and ever he wept as he had been a child. With that came his mother, the Queen of Orkney, and when she saw Sir Gareth really face to face she suddenly fell down in a swoon. Then Sir Gareth comforted his mother in such a wise that she recovered, and made good cheer. And the Lady Liones came, among all the ladies there named the fairest and peerless. And there the King asked his nephew Sir Gareth whether he would have that lady to his wife.

"My lord," said he, "wit ye well that I love her above all ladies."

"Now, fair lady," said King Arthur, "what say ye?"

"Most noble King," said Dame Liones, "wit ye well that my Lord Gareth is to me more dear to have and to hold as my husband than any king or prince that is christened, and if ye will suffer him to have his will and free choice, I dare say he will have me."

"That is truth," said Sir Gareth, "and if I have not you and hold not you as my wife I wed no lady."

"What, nephew," said the King, "is the wind in that door! Wit ye well I would not for the stint of my crown be causer to withdraw your hearts. Ye shall have my love and my lordship in the uttermost wise that may lie in my power."

Then was there made a provision for the day of marriage, and by the King's advice it should be at Michaelmas following at Kink-Kenadon by the seaside. And when the day came the Bishop of Canterbury made the wedding betwixt Sir Gareth and the Lady Liones with great solemnity. And at the same time Gaheris was wedded to Linet.

When this solemnisation was done there came in the Green Knight, the Red Knight, and all the others that had yielded themselves to Sir Gareth, and did homage and fealty to hold their lands of him for ever, and desired to serve him at the feast. And the kings and queens, princes, earls, and barons, and many bold knights went unto meat, and well may ye wit that there was all manner of meat plenteously, all manner of revels, and games, with all manner of minstrelsy that was used in those days. So they held the court forty days with great solemnity.

And this Sir Gareth was a noble knight, and a well ruled, and fair languaged.

How Young Tristram Saved the Life of the Queen of Lyonesse

There was a king called Meliodas, as likely a knight as any living, and he was lord of the country of Lyonesse. At that time King Arthur reigned supreme over England, Wales, Scotland, and many other realms, howbeit there were many lords of countries that held their lands under King Arthur. So also was the King of France subject to him, and the King of Brittany, and all the lordships as far as Rome. The wife of this King Meliodas was a full good and fair lady, called Elizabeth, the sister of King Mark of Cornwall. Well she loved her lord, and he her again, and there was much joy betwixt them. There was a lady in that country who bore ill will towards this king and queen, and therefore upon a day, as he rode on hunting, for he was a great chaser, she by an enchantment made him chase a hart by himself alone till he came to an old castle, where anon she had him taken prisoner.

When Queen Elizabeth missed her lord she was nigh out of her wit, and she took a gentlewoman with her and ran into the forest to seek him. When she was far in the forest and might go no farther, she sank down exhausted. For the default of help she took cold there, and she soon knew that she must die. So she begged her gentlewoman to commend her to King Meliodas, and to say that she was full sorry to depart out of this world from him, and that their little child, that was to have such sorrow even in his infancy, should be christened Tristram.

Therewith this queen gave up the ghost and died. The gentlewoman laid her under the shadow of a great tree, and right so there came the barons, following after the queen. When they saw that she was dead they had her carried home, and much dole[1] was made for her.

The morn after his queen died King Meliodas was delivered out of prison, and the sorrow he made for her, when he was come home, no tongue might tell. He had her richly interred, and afterwards, as she had commanded afore her death, had his child christened Tristram, the sorrowful born child. For seven years he remained without a wife, and all that time young Tristram was nourished well.

Then, when he wedded King Howell's daughter of Brittany and had other children, the stepmother was wroth that Tristram should be heir to the country of Lyonesse rather than her own son. Wherefore this jealous queen resolved to become rid of her stepson, and she put poison into a silver cup in the chamber where Tristram and her children were together, intending that when Tristram was thirsty he should drink it. But it happened that the queen's own son espied the cup with poison, and, because the child was thirsty and supposed it was good drink, he took of it freely. Therewithal he died suddenly, and when the queen wist of the death of her son, wit ye well that she was heavy of heart. But yet the king understood nothing of her treason.

Notwithstanding all this the queen would not leave her jealousy, and soon had more poison put in a cup. By fortune King Meliodas, her husband, found the cup where was the poison, and being much thirsty he took to drink thereout. Anon the queen espied him and ran unto him and pulled the cup from him suddenly. The king marvelled why she did so, and remembered how her son was suddenly slain with poison. Then he took her by the hand, and said: "Thou false traitress, thou shalt tell me what manner of drink this is." Therewith he pulled out his sword, and swore a great oath that he should slay her if she told him not the truth.

Then she told him all, and by the assent of the barons she was condemned to be burned as a traitress, according to the law. A great fire was made, and just as she was at the fire to take her execution young Tristram kneeled afore King Meliodas and besought of him a boon. "I grant it," said the king, whereupon the youth demanded the life of the queen, his stepmother.

"That is unrightfully asked," said King Melodias, "for she would have slain thee, if she had had her will, and for thy sake most is my cause that she should die."

But Tristram besought his father to forgive her, as he himself did, and required him to hold his promise. Then said the king, "Since ye will have it so, I give her to you; go ye to the fire and take her, and do with her what ye will."

So Sir Tristram went to the fire, and by the commandment of the king delivered her from death. But thereafter King Meliodas would never have aught to do with her, though by the good means of young Tristram he at length forgave her. Ever after in her life she never hated her stepson more, but loved him and had great joy of him, because he saved her from the fire. But the king would not suffer him to abide longer at his court.

[1] Dole: sorrow; mourning.

Sir Tristram's First Battle

King Melodias sought out a gentleman that was well learned, and taught, and with him, named Gouvernail, he sent young Tristram away from Lyonesse court into France, to learn the language and customs and deeds of arms. There he learned to be a harper passing all others of his time, and he also applied himself well to the gentlemanly art of hawking and hunting, for he that gentle is will draw unto him gentle qualities and follow the customs of noble gentlemen. The old chronicle saith he adopted good methods for the chase, and the terms he used we have yet in hawking and hunting. Therefore the book of forest sports is called the Book of Sir Tristram.

When he well could speak the language and had learned all that he might in that country, he came home again, and remained in Cornwall until he was big and strong, of the age of nineteen years, and his father, King Meliodas, had great joy of him.

Then it befell that King Anguish of Ireland sent to King Mark of Cornwall for the tribute long paid him, but now seven years behind. King Mark and his barons gave unto the messenger of Ireland the answer that they would no tribute pay, and bade him tell his king that if he wished tribute he should send a trusty knight of his land to fight for it against another that Cornwall should find to defend its right. With this the messenger departed into Ireland.

When King Anguish understood the answer, he was wonderfully wroth, and called unto him Sir Marhaus, the good and proved knight, brother unto the queen of Ireland, and a knight of the Round Table, and said to him: "Fair brother, I pray you go into Cornwall for my sake, and do battle for the tribute that of right we ought to have."

Sir Marhaus was not loath to do battle for his king and his land, and in all haste he was fitted with all things that to him needed, and so he departed out of Ireland and arrived in Cornwall even fast by the castle of Tintagil.

When King Mark understood that the good and noble knight Sir Marhaus was come to fight for Ireland, he made great sorrow, for he knew no knight that durst have ado with him. Sir Marhaus remained on his ship, and every day he sent word unto King Mark that he should pay the tribute or else find a champion to fight for it with him.

Then they of Cornwall let make cries in every place, that what knight would fight to save the tribute should be rewarded so that he should fare the better the term of his life. But no one came to do the battle, and some counselled King Mark to send to the court of King Arthur to seek Sir Launcelot of the Lake, that at that time was named for the marvellousest knight of all the world. Others said it were labour in vain to do so, because Sir Marhaus was one of the knights of the Round Table, and any one of them would be loath to have ado with other. So the king and all his barons at the last agreed that it was no boot to seek any knight of the Round Table.

Meanwhile came the language and the noise unto young Tristram how Sir Marhaus abode battle fast by Tintagil, and how King Mark could find no manner of knight to fight for him. Then Sir Tristram was wroth and sore ashamed that there durst no knight in Cornwall have ado with Sir Marhaus, and he went unto his father, King Meliodas, and said: "Alas, that I am not made knight; if I were, I would engage with him. I pray you give me leave to ride to King Mark to be made knight by him."

"I will well," said the father, "that ye be ruled as your courage will rule you."

So Tristram went unto his uncle, who quickly gave him the order of knighthood, and anon sent a messenger unto Sir Marhaus with letters that said he had found a young knight ready to take the battle to the uttermost. Then in all haste King Mark had Sir Tristram horsed and armed in the best manner that might be had or gotten for gold or silver, and he was put into a vessel, both his horse and he, and all that to him belonged both for his body and for his horse, to be taken to an island nigh Sir Marhaus' ships, where it was agreed that they should fight. And when King Mark and his barons beheld young Sir Tristram depart to fight for the right of Cornwall, there was neither man nor woman of honour but wept to see so young a knight jeopard himself for their right.

When Sir Tristram was arrived at the island, he commanded his servant Gouvernail to bring his horse to the land and to dress his horse rightly, and then, when he was in the saddle well apparelled and his shield dressed upon his shoulder, he commanded Gouvernail to go to his vessel again and return to King Mark. "And upon thy life," said he, "come thou not nigh this island till thou see me overcome or slain, or else that I win yonder knight." So either departed from other.

When Sir Marhaus perceived this young knight seeking to encounter with himself, one of the most renowned knights of the world, he said, "Fair sir, since thou hopest to win honour of me, I let thee wit honour mayest thou none lose by me if thou mayest stand me three strokes, for I let thee wit for my noble deeds, proved and seen, King Arthur made me knight of the Table Round."

Then they put spears in rest and ran together so fiercely that they smote either other down, horse and all. Anon they pulled out their swords and lashed together as men that were wild and courageous. Thus they fought more than half a day, and either was wounded passing sore, so that the blood ran down freshly from them upon the ground. By then Sir Tristram waxed more fresh than Sir Marhaus, and better winded, and bigger, and with a mighty stroke he smote Sir Marhaus upon the helm such a buffet, that it went through his helm and through the coif of steel and through the brain-pan, and the sword stuck so fast in the helm and in his brain-pan that Sir Tristram pulled thrice at his sword or ever he might pull it out from his head; and there Marhaus fell down on his knees, the edge of Tristram's sword left in his brain-pan. Suddenly Sir Marhaus rose grovelling, and threw his sword and his shield from him, and so ran to his ships and fled his way, sore groaning.

Anon he and his fellowship departed into Ireland, and, as soon as he came to the king his brother, he had his wounds searched, and in his head was found a piece of Sir Tristram's sword. No surgeons might cure this wound, and so he died of Sir Tristram's sword. That piece of the sword the queen his sister kept ever with her, for she thought to be revenged, if she might.

Now turn we again unto Sir Tristram, that was sore wounded by a spear-thrust of Sir Marhaus so that he might scarcely stir. He sat down softly upon a little hill, and bled fast. Then anon came Gouvernail, his man, with his vessel, and Sir Tristram was quickly taken back into the castle of Tintagil. He was cared for in the best manner possible, but he lay there a month and more, and ever he was like to die of the stroke from Sir Marhaus' spear, for, as the French book saith, the spear's head was envenomed. Then was King Mark passing heavy, and he sent after all manner of surgeons, but there was none that would promise him life.

At last there came a right wise lady, and she said plainly that he should never be whole unless he went into the same country that the venom came from, and in that country he should be holpen, or else never. When King Mark understood that, he let provide for Sir Tristram a fair vessel, well victualled, and therein was put Sir Tristram and Gouvernail, with him. Sir Tristram took his harp with him, and so they put to sea to sail into Ireland.

Sir Tristram and the Fair Isoud

By good fortune Sir Tristram with Gouvernail arrived in Ireland fast by a castle where King Anguish and the queen were. As he came to land he sat and harped in his bed a merry lay, such as none in Ireland ever heard afore that time. And when the king and queen were told of this stranger that was such a harper, anon they sent for him and let search his wounds, and then asked him his name. Then he answered, "I am of the country of Lyonesse; my name is Tramtrist, and I was thus wounded in a battle, as I fought for a lady's right."

"Truly," said King Anguish, "ye shall have all the help in this land that ye may. But I let you wit in Cornwall I had a great loss as ever king had, for there I lost the best knight of the world. His name was Marhaus, a full noble knight of the Table Round." Then he told Sir Tristram wherefore Sir Marhaus was slain. Sir Tristram made semblant as if he were sorry, and yet better knew he how it was than the king.

The king for great favour had Tramtrist put in his daughter's keeping, because she was a noble surgeon. When she searched his wound she found that therein was poison, and so she healed him within a while. Therefore Tramtrist cast great devotion to the Fair Isoud, for she was at that time the fairest maid of the world. He taught her to harp, and she soon began to have a great fancy unto him. Then soon he showed himself to be so brave and true a knight in the jousts that she had great suspicion that he was some man of honour proved, and she loved him more than heretofore.

Thus was Sir Tramtrist long there well cherished by the king and the queen and especially by Isoud the Fair. Upon a day as Sir Tramtrist was absent, the queen and Isoud roamed up and down in the chamber, and beheld his sword there as it lay upon his bed. And then by mishap the queen drew out the sword and regarded it a long while. Both thought it a passing fair sword, but within a foot and a half of the point there was a great piece thereof broken out of the edge. When the queen espied that gap in the sword, she remembered her of a piece of a sword that was found in the brain-pan of Sir Marhaus, her brother. "Alas," then said she unto her daughter, the Fair Isoud, "this is the traitor knight that slew thine uncle."

When Isoud heard her say so she was sore abashed, for much she loved Sir Tramtrist, and full well she knew the cruelness of her mother. Anon the queen went unto her own chamber and sought her coffer, and there she took out the piece of the sword that was pulled out of Sir Marhaus' head. Then she ran with that piece of iron to the sword that lay upon the bed, and when she put that piece unto the sword, it was as meet as it could be when new broken. The queen now gripped that sword in her hand fiercely, and with all her might ran straight to where she knew Tramtrist was, and there she would have thrust him through, had not a knight pulled the sword from her.

Then when she was letted of her evil will, she ran to King Anguish and told him on her knees what traitor he had in his house. The king was right heavy thereof, but charged the queen to leave him to deal with the knight. He went straight into the chamber unto Sir Tramtrist, that he found by now all ready armed to mount upon his horse. King Anguish saw that it was of no avail to fight, and that it was no honour to slay Sir Tramtrist while a guest within his court; so he gave him leave to depart from Ireland in safety, if he would tell who he was, and whether he slew Sir Marhaus.

"Sir," said Tristram, "now I shall tell you all the truth: My father's name is Meliodas, king of Lyonesse, and my mother is called Elizabeth, that was sister unto King Mark of Cornwall. I was christened Tristram, but, because I would not be known in this country, I turned my name, and had myself called Tramtrist. For the tribute of Cornwall I fought for mine uncle's sake, and for the right of Cornwall that ye had possessed many years. And wit ye well I did the battle for the love of mine uncle, King Mark, for the love of the country of Cornwall, and to increase mine honour."

"Truly," said the king, "I may not say but ye did as a knight should; howbeit I may not maintain you in this country with my honour."

"Sir," said Tristram, "I thank you for your good lordship that I have had with you here, and the great goodness my lady your daughter hath shown me. It may so happen that ye shall win more by my life than by my death, for in the parts of England it may be I may do you service at some season so that ye shall be glad that ever ye showed me your good lordship. I beseech your good grace that I may take my leave of your daughter and of all the barons and knights."

This request the king granted, and Sir Tristram went unto the Fair Isoud and took leave of her. And he told her all,—what he was, how he had changed his name because he would not be known, and how a lady told him that he should never be whole till he came into this country where the poison was made. She was full woe of his departing, and wept heartily.

"Madam," said Tristram, "I promise you faithfully that I shall be all the days of my life your knight."

"Grammercy," said the Fair Isoud, "and I promise you against that I shall not be married this seven years but by your assent."

Then Sir Tristram gave her a ring, and she gave him another, and therewith he departed from her, leaving her making great dole and lamentation. And he straight went unto the court among all the barons, and there he took his leave of most and least, and so departed and took the sea, and with good wind he arrived up at Tintagil in Cornwall.

How Sir Tristram Demanded the Fair Isoud for King Mark, and How Sir Tristram and Isoud Drank the Love Potion

When there came tidings that Sir Tristram was arrived and whole of his wounds, King Mark was passing glad, and so were all the barons. And Sir Tristram lived at the court of King Mark in great joy long time, until at the last there befell a jealousy and an unkindness between them. Then King Mark cast always in his heart how he might destroy Sir Tristram.

The beauty and goodness of the Fair Isoud were so praised by Sir Tristram that King Mark said he would wed her, and prayed Sir Tristram to take his way into Ireland for him, as his messenger, to bring her to Cornwall. All this was done to the intent to slay Sir Tristram. Notwithstanding, Sir Tristram would not refuse the message for any danger or peril, and made ready to go in the goodliest wise that might be devised. He took with him the goodliest knights that he might find in the court, arrayed them after the guise that was then used, and so departed over sea with all his fellowship.

Anon as he was in the broad sea a tempest took them and drove them back into the coast of England. They came to land fast by Camelot, and there Sir Tristram set up his pavilion. Now it fell that King Anguish of Ireland was accused of slaying by treason a cousin of Sir Launcelot of the Lake, and just at this time he was come to the court at the summoning of King Arthur upon pain of forfeiture of his lands; yet ere he arrived at Camelot he wist not wherefore he was sent after. When he heard the accusation he understood full well there was no remedy but to answer it knightly, for the custom was in those days, that if any man were accused of any treason or murder, he should fight body for body or else find another knight to fight for him. Now King Anguish grew passing heavy when he heard his accusing, for the knights of King Ban's blood, as Sir Launcelot was, were as hard men to win in battle as any then living.

The meanwhile Sir Tristram was told how King Anguish was come thither in great distress, and he sent Gouvernail to bring him to his pavilion. When Sir Tristram saw the king coming he ran unto him and would have holden his stirrup, but King Anguish leaped lightly from his horse, and either embraced other heartily. Sir Tristram remembered his promise, made when departing from Ireland, to do service to King Anguish if ever it lay in his power, and never had there been so great need of knight's help as now. So when King Anguish told Sir Tristram all, Sir Tristram took the battle for the sake of the good lordship showed him in Ireland, and for the sake of the Fair Isoud, upon the condition that King Anguish grant two things. One was that he should swear that he was in the right and had never consented to the death of the knight. The second request was to be granted after the battle, if God should speed him therein.

King Anguish quickly granted Sir Tristram whatsoever he asked, and anon departed unto King Arthur's judges, and told them he had found a champion ready to do the battle for him. So Sir Tristram fought for King Anguish and overcame his adversary, a most noble knight. Then King Anguish and Sir Tristram joyfully took their leave, and sailed into Ireland with great nobleness.

When they were in Ireland the king let make it known throughout all the land, how and in what manner Sir Tristram had done for him. Then the queen and all that were there made the most of him that they might. But the joy that the Fair Isoud made of Sir Tristram no tongue might tell, for of men earthly she loved him most.

Then upon a day King Anguish would know from Sir Tristram why he asked not his boon, for whatsoever had been promised he should have without fail. "Sir," said Tristram, "now is it time, and this is what I desire: that ye will give me the Fair Isoud, your daughter, not for myself, but for mine uncle, King Mark, that shall have her to wife, for so have I promised him."

"Alas," said the king, "I had rather than all the land that I have ye would wed her yourself."

"Sir," said Sir Tristram, "if I did, then were I ashamed for ever in this world, and false of my promise. Therefore I pray you hold your promise that ye gave me, for this is my desire, that ye will give me the Fair Isoud to go with me into Cornwall, to be wedded to King Mark, mine uncle."

[Illustration: Sir Tristram and the Fair Isoud]

"As for that," said King Anguish, "ye shall have her with you, to do with her what it please you; that is to say, if ye list to wed her yourself, that is to me lievest[1]; and if ye will give her unto King Mark, that is in your choice."

So, to make a short conclusion, the Fair Isoud was made ready to go with Sir Tristram, and Dame Bragwaine went with her for her chief gentlewoman, with many others. The queen, Isoud's mother, gave to Dame Bragwaine and unto Gouvernail a drink, and charged them that what day King Mark should wed, that same day they should give him that drink, "and then," said the queen, "I undertake either shall love other the days of their life."

So this drink was given unto Dame Bragwaine and unto Gouvernail, and then anon Sir Tristram took the sea with the Fair Isoud. When they were in the cabin, it happened that they were thirsty, and they saw a little flask of gold stand by them, that seemed by the colour and the taste to be noble wine. Then Sir Tristram took the flask in his hand, and said: "Madam Isoud, here is the best drink that ever ye drank, that Dame Bragwaine your maid and Gouvernail my servant have kept for themselves."

Then they laughed and made good cheer, and either drank to other, thinking never drink was so sweet or so good. But after they had drunk that magic wine, they loved either other so truly that never their love departed either for weal or for woe.

So they sailed on till by fortune they came into Cornwall. There all the barons met them, and anon King Mark and the Fair Isoud were richly wedded with great splendour. But ever, as the French book saith, Sir Tristram and the Fair Isoud loved each other truly, and his life long he was her loyal and honourable knight.

[1] Lievest: dearest.

How Sir Tristram Departed from Tintagil, and Was Long in the Forest

There were great jousts and tourneying at that time in Cornwall, and Sir Tristram was most praised of all the knights. But some were jealous because of his prowess, and especially Sir Andred, that was cousin unto Sir Tristram, ever lay in a watch to wait betwixt him and the Fair Isoud, for to take them and slander them. So upon a day Sir Tristram talked with Isoud in a window, and that espied Sir Andred, and told it to the king.

Then King Mark took a sword in his hand and came to Sir Tristram, and called him false traitor, and would have stricken him. But Sir Tristram ran under his sword, and took it out of his hand. And then the king cried, "Where are my knights and my men? I charge you slay this traitor."

But there was not one would move for his words. When Sir Tristram saw there was not one would be against him, he shook the sword to the king, and made as though he would strike him. And then King Mark fled, for he was a coward, and Sir Tristram followed him, and smote upon him five or six strokes with the flat of his sword on the neck so that he made him fall upon the nose. Sir Tristram then went his way and armed himself, and took his horse and his man, and so he rode into the forest.

King Mark called his council unto him and asked advice of his barons what was best to do with Sir Tristram. Their counsel was to send for him, that they might be friends, for in a quarrel, if Sir Tristram were hard bestead, many men would hold with him against the king; and if so peerless a knight should depart from King Mark's court and go to King Arthur's he would get himself such friends there that Cornwall would be in ill repute.

So the barons sent for Sir Tristram under a safe conduct, and he was welcomed back by King Mark. But his enemies ever plotted against him, and on a day Sir Andred and some of the barons set upon him secretly, seized him, and took him, bound hand and foot, unto a chapel which stood upon the sea rocks. When Sir Tristram saw that Andred meant to kill him there, he said: "Fair Lords, remember what I have done for the country Cornwall, and in what jeopardy I have been for the weal of you all, and see not me die thus to the shame of all knighthood."

But Andred held to his purpose, and when Sir Tristram saw him draw his sword to kill him, he looked upon both his hands that were fast bound unto two knights, and suddenly he pulled them both to him and so freed his hands. Then he leaped unto his cousin Andred and wrested his sword out of his hands. Then he smote Sir Andred to the earth, and fought with the others till he had killed ten knights. So Sir Tristram gat the chapel and kept it by force.

Then the uproar became great, and the people gathered unto Sir Andred, more than a hundred, whereupon Sir Tristram shut fast the chapel door, and brake the bars of a window, and so he leaped out and fell upon the crags by the sea. Here Sir Andred and his fellows might not get to him at that time, and so they departed.

When Sir Tristram's men heard that he was escaped they were passing glad, and on the rocks they found him, and with towels they pulled him up. Then Sir Tristram dreaded sore lest he were discovered unto the king, wherefore he sent Gouvernail for his horse and his spear, and so he rode his way into the forest. As he rode he was in great sorrow at departing in this wise; and there, as he made great dole, by fortune a damsel met him, and she and her lady brought him meat and drink. Also they brought him a harp, for they knew him, and wist that for goodly harping he bore the prize in the world.

So they tried to give him comfort, but he ate little of the food, and at the last, came wholly out his mind for sorrow. He would go about in the wilderness breaking down the trees and boughs; and otherwhile, when he found the harp that the lady sent him, then would he harp and play thereupon and weep together. Sometimes when Sir Tristram was in the wood, then would the lady sit down and play upon the harp; then would he come to that harp and hearken thereto, and sometimes he would harp himself.

Thus it went on a quarter of a year, when at the last Sir Tristram ran his way, and the lady wist not what had become of him. He waxed lean and poor of flesh, and fell into the fellowship of herdmen and shepherds, and daily they would give him of their meat and drink. And when he did any evil deed they would beat him with rods, and so they clipped him with shears and made him like a fool.

And upon a day Sir Dagonet, King Arthur's fool, came into Cornwall, with two squires with him, and as they rode through the forest they came by a fair well where Sir Tristram was wont to be. The weather was hot, and they alighted to drink of that well, and in the meanwhile their horses brake loose. Just then Sir Tristram came unto them, and first he soused Sir Dagonet in that well, and then his squires, and thereat laughed the shepherds. Forthwithal he ran after their horses, and brought them again one by one, and right so, wet as they were, he made Sir Dagonet and his squires mount and ride their ways.

Thus Sir Tristram endured there a half-year, and would never come in town or village. Then Sir Andred, that was cousin unto Sir Tristram, let a tale be brought unto King Mark's court that Sir Tristram was dead, and that ere he died he besought King Mark to make Sir Andred king of the country of Lyonesse, of the which Sir Tristram was lord. When Queen Isoud heard of these tidings she made such sorrow that she was nigh out of her mind, and she lay long sick, at the point of death.

Meanwhile a knight came unto King Mark and told him of a mad man in the forest at the fair fountain. So he commanded his knights to take Sir Tristram with fairness, and bring him to his castle, yet he knew not that the mad man was Sir Tristram. They did softly and fair, and cast mantles upon Sir Tristram, and so led him unto Tintagil. There they bathed him, and gave him hot suppings, till they had brought him well to his remembrance. But all this while there was no creature that knew Sir Tristram, nor what man he was.

Now it fell upon a day that the queen, the Fair Isoud, heard of this man that ran wild in the forest and how the king had brought him home to the court, and with Dame Bragwaine she went to see him in the garden, where he was reposing in the sun. When she looked upon Sir Tristram she knew not that it was he, yet it seemed to her she had seen him before. But as soon as Sir Tristram saw her he knew her well enough, and he turned away his visage and wept. The queen had always with her a little dog that Sir Tristram gave her the first time that ever she came into Cornwall, and never would that dog depart from her unless Sir Tristram was nigh there with Isoud. Anon as this little dog caught a scent of Sir Tristram, she leaped upon him, licked his cheeks, whined and smelled at his feet and over his whole body. Then the Fair Isoud saw that it was her lord, Sir Tristram, and thereupon she fell down in a swoon, and so lay a great while.

When she might speak, she blessed God that Sir Tristram was still alive, yet she knew that her lord King Mark would discover him by the little dog that would never leave him.

How King Mark Was Sorry for the Good Renown of Sir Tristram

The queen departed from Sir Tristram but the little dog would not from him. Therewithal came King Mark, and the dog set upon him and bayed at all the barons. Thereupon Sir Andred saw by the dog that it was Sir Tristram, and King Mark repented that he had brought the mad man in from the forest. Then he let call his barons to judge Sir Tristram to death. They would not assent thereto, but by the advice of them all he was banished out of the country for ten years.

So Sir Tristram was made to depart out of the country of Cornwall, and there were many barons brought him into his ship. When he was ready to set sail he said: "Greet well King Mark and all mine enemies, and say I will come again when I may. And well am I rewarded for the fighting with Sir Marhaus, and delivering all this country from servage, and well am I rewarded for the fetching of the Fair Isoud out of Ireland, and the danger I was in first and last."

So Sir Tristram departed over sea, and arrived in Wales. As he rode there through the Forest Perilous, a lady in great distress met him, that said: "O my lord, come with me, and that in all the haste ye may, for ye shall see the most honourable knight of the world hard bestead, and he is none other than the noble King Arthur himself."

"God defend," said Sir Tristram, "that ever he should be in such distress. I am ready to help him if I may."

So they rode at a great pace, till they saw a knight, that was King Arthur, on foot fighting with two knights, and anon the one knight was smitten down, and they unlaced his helm to slay him. Therewithal came Sir Tristram with all his might, and smote the two traitors so that they fell dead. Then he horsed King Arthur, and as they rode forth together, the King thanked heartily Sir Tristram and desired to wit his name. He would not tell him, but said that he was a poor knight adventurous. So he bare King Arthur fellowship, till he met with some of his knights.

Then departed Sir Tristram, and rode straight toward Camelot. Then was he ware of a seemly knight riding against him with a covered shield. They dressed their shields and spears, and came together with all the mights of their horses. They met so fiercely that both horses and knights fell to the earth. As fast as they were able they then gat free from their horses, and put their shields before them; and they strake together with bright swords, like men of might, and either wounded other wonderly sore, so that the blood ran out upon the grass.

Thus they two fought the space of four hours. Never one would speak to other one word, and of their harness they hewed off many pieces. Then at the last spake the one with the covered shield; "Knight, thou fightest wonderly well as ever I saw knight; therefore if it please you tell me your name."

"Sir," said Sir Tristram, "that is me loath to tell any man my name."

"Truly," said the other, "if I was requested, I was never loath to tell my name. I am Sir Launcelot of the Lake."

"Alas," said Sir Tristram, "what have I done, for ye are the man in the world that I love best."

"Fair knight," said Sir Launcelot, "tell me now your name."

"Truly," said he, "my name is Sir Tristram of Lyonesse."

"Oh," said Sir Launcelot, "what adventure is befallen me!"

Therewith Sir Launcelot kneeled adown, and yielded him up his sword. And therewithal Sir Tristram kneeled adown, and yielded him up his sword. So either gave other the victory. Thereupon they both forthwithal went to a stone, and sat down upon it, and took off their helms to cool themselves. Then after a while they took their helms and rode together to Camelot.

There soon they met King Arthur, and when he wist that it was Sir Tristram, he ran unto him and took him by the hand and said, "Sir Tristram, ye be as welcome as any knight that ever came to this court." Then they went to the Table Round, where Queen Guenever came, and many ladies with her, and all the ladies said at one voice, "Welcome, Sir Tristram." "Welcome," said the damsels; "Welcome," said the knights; "Welcome," said Arthur, "for one of the best knights and the gentlest of the world, and the man of most honour. For of all manner of hunting ye bear the prize; and of all the terms of hunting and hawking ye are the beginner; of all instruments of music ye are the best. Therefore, gentle knight, ye are welcome to this court. Now I pray you, grant me a boon."

"It shall be at your commandment," said Tristram.

"Well," said Arthur, "I will desire of you that ye will abide in my court."

"Sir," said Sir Tristram, "thereto is me loath, for I have ado in many countries."

"Not so," said Arthur; "ye have promised it me, and ye may not say nay."

So Tristram agreed to remain with King Arthur, who then went unto the sieges about the Round Table, and looked in every siege that lacked a knight. Then the King saw in the siege of Marhaus letters that said, "This is the siege of the noble knight Sir Tristram." And then Arthur made Sir Tristram knight of the Table Round with great splendour and great feast, as might be thought. For that Sir Marhaus, a worthy knight, was slain afore by the hands of Sir Tristram was well known at that time in the court of Arthur; and that for evil deeds that he did unto the country of Cornwall Sir Tristram and he fought; and that they fought so long tracing and traversing till they fell bleeding to the earth, for they were so sore wounded that they might not stand; and that Sir Tristram by fortune recovered, and Sir Marhaus died through the stroke on the head.

King Mark had had great despite of the renown of Sir Tristram, and therefore had chased him out of Cornwall. When now he heard of the great prowess that Sir Tristram did in England he was sore grieved, and sent men to espy what deeds he did. The Queen Isoud also on her part sent privily spies to know what deeds he had done, for great love was between them twain. When the messengers came home, and told that Sir Tristram passed all other knights at Arthur's court unless it were Sir Launcelot, King Mark was right heavy of the tidings, and as glad was the Fair Isoud. Then in great despite King Mark took with him two good knights and two squires, disguised himself, and took his way into England, to the intent to slay Sir Tristram.

So King Mark came into England, where he soon became known as the most horrible coward that ever bestrode horse; and there was much laughing and jesting at the knight of Cornwall, and much he was despised. Sir Dagonet, King Arthur's fool, at one time chased him through thick and thin over the forests; and when on a day Sir Launcelot overtook him and bade him turn and fight, he made no defence, but tumbled down out off the saddle to the earth as a sack, and there he lay still, and cried Sir Launcelot mercy.

So King Mark was soon brought as recreant before King Arthur, who already knew wherefore he was come into his country, and that he had not done the service and homage he owed as King Arthur's under-lord. But King Mark promised to make large amends for the wrongs he had done, for he was a fair speaker, and false thereunder. So on a day King Arthur prayed of him one gift, and King Mark promised to give him whatsoever he desired, if it were in his power. Then King Arthur asked him to be good lord unto Sir Tristram, and to take him back into Cornwall, and to cherish him for Arthur's sake. King Mark promised this, and swore upon a book afore Arthur and all his knights. Therewith King Arthur forgave him all the evil will that ever he owed him, and King Mark and Sir Tristram took either other by the hands hard knit together. But for all this King Mark thought falsely, as it proved afterward.

Then soon afterward King Mark took his leave to ride into Cornwall, and Sir Tristram rode with him; wherefore the most part of the Round Table were passing heavy, and some were wroth, knowing that King Mark was the most coward and the villainest knight living.

After a while letters came out of Cornwall that spake ill of Sir Tristram and showed plainly that King Mark took Sir Tristram for his mortal enemy. Sir Launcelot in especial made great sorrow for anger, wherefore Dinadan, a gentle, wise, and courteous knight, said to him: "King Mark is so villainous that by fair speech shall never man get of him. But ye shall see what I shall do. I will make a lay for him, and when it is made I shall make a harper sing it afore him."

So anon Dinadan went and made the lay, hoping thereby to humble the crafty king; and he taught it an harper named Eliot, and when he knew it, he taught it to many harpers. And so, by the will of Sir Launcelot and of Arthur, the harpers went straight into Wales and into Cornwall, to sing the lay that Sir Dinadan made of King Mark, which was the worst lay that ever harper sang with harp or with any other instrument.

At a great feast that King Mark made came in Eliot the harper, and because he was a curious harper, men heard him sing the lay that Dinadan had made, the which spake the most villainy of King Mark's treason that ever man heard. When the harper had sung his song to the end, King Mark was wonderly wroth, for he deemed that the lay that was sung afore him was made by Sir Tristram's counsel, wherefore he thought to slay him and all his well willers in that country.

So King Mark grew ever more jealous of Sir Tristram because of his prowess as knight and his great love and loyal devotion to the queen, the Fair Isoud; and by treason King Mark let take him and put him in prison, contrary to his promise that he made unto King Arthur. When Queen Isoud understood that Sir Tristram was in prison, she made as great sorrow as ever made lady or gentlewoman. Then Sir Tristram sent a letter unto her, and prayed her to be his good lady; and if it pleased her to make a vessel ready for her and him, he would go with her unto the realm of Logris, that is this land.

When the Fair Isoud understood Sir Tristram's letter and his intent, she sent him another, and bade him be of good comfort, for she would make the vessel ready, and all things to purpose. Then she had King Mark taken and put in prison, until the time that she and Sir Tristram were departed unto the realm of Logris. And then Sir Tristram was delivered out of prison, and anon in all haste they took their vessel, and came by water into England.

When Sir Launcelot understood that Sir Tristram was there, he was full glad. He espied whither he went, and after him he rode, and then either made of other great joy. And so Sir Launcelot brought Sir Tristram and the Fair Isoud unto Joyous Gard, that was Sir Launcelot's own castle that he had won with his own hands. And he charged all his people to honour them and love them as they would do himself.

Near three years Sir Tristram kept the Fair Isoud with him in Joyous Gard, and then by means of treaties he brought her again unto King Fox, which was the name Sir Launcelot gave unto Mark because of his wiles and treason. But ever the malice of King Fox followed his brave nephew, and in the end he slew him as he sat harping afore his lady, the Fair Isoud, with a trenchant glaive, thrust in behind to the heart.

For his death was much bewailing of every knight that ever was in Arthur's days, for he was traitorously slain. And the Fair Isoud died, swooning upon the cross of Sir Tristram, whereof was great pity. And all that were with King Mark that were consenting to the death of Sir Tristram were slain, as Sir Andred and many others.

How Sir Percivale of Galis Sought and Found Sir Launcelot

While King Arthur and his knights were still sorrowful over Sir Tristram's return to Cornwall, greatly fearing mischief to the good knight by some manner of falsehood or treason of King Mark, there came to the court a knight bringing a young squire with him. It was Sir Aglovale, King Pellinore's son, and the squire was his brother, Percivale, that he wished King Arthur to make knight. The boy was the youngest of five sons, and for love of the father and the brothers, good knights all, the King made him a knight the next day in Camelot; yet the King and all the knights thought it would be long ere he proved a man of prowess, and Sir Kay and Sir Mordred made sport of his rude manner.

At the dinner, when every knight was set after his honour, the King commanded Sir Percivale to be placed among mean knights. But there was a maiden in the Queen's court that was come of high blood, yet she was dumb, and never spake a word. Right so she came straight into the hall, went unto Sir Percivale, took him by the hand, and said aloud, that the King and all the knights might hear it, "Arise, Sir Percivale, the noble knight and God's knight, and go with me."

So he did, and she brought him to the right side of the Siege Perilous, and said, "Fair knight, take here thy siege, for that siege appertaineth to thee, and to none other." Right so she departed, and soon afterward she died. Then the King and all the court made great joy of Sir Percivale.

Then Sir Percivale rode forth upon adventures, and came unto Cornwall to seek Sir Tristram. And he delivered him from a prison where King Mark had placed him, and then rode straight unto King Mark and told him he had done himself great shame to treat so falsely Sir Tristram, the knight of most renown in all the world. Then Sir Percivale departed, but anon King Mark bethought him of more treason, notwithstanding his promise never by any manner of means to hurt Sir Tristram, and he let take him and put him again in prison. How he then escaped with Isoud into England we have already read in the tale of Sir Tristram.

Now it chanced that Sir Launcelot of the Lake had sore offended the Queen Guenever, and she rebuked him harshly, called him false traitor knight, and sent him from her court. Therewith he took such an hearty sorrow at her words that he went clean out of his mind, and leaped out at a bay window into a garden, and there with thorns he was all scratched up in his visage. So he ran forth he wist not whither, and for a long while none of his kin wist what was become of him.

Soon Queen Guenever was right sorry that she had been so angry with her faithful knight, and on her knees besought Sir Bors and many others to seek Sir Launcelot throughout all England, Wales, and Scotland. So these noble knights by one assent rode forth by twos and threes; and ever they assigned where they should meet.

Sir Aglovale and Sir Percivale rode together unto their mother that was a queen in those days. And when she saw her two sons, for joy she wept tenderly and said, "Ah my dear sons, when your father was slain he left me five sons, of the which now be three slain; my heart shall never be glad more." Then she kneeled down tofore Aglovale and Percivale, and besought them to abide at home with her.

"Ah, sweet mother," said Sir Percivale, "we may not, for we be come of king's blood on both sides, and therefore, mother, it is our kind to follow arms and noble deeds."

Then there was but weeping and sobbing when they should depart, and after they were gone, she sent a squire after them with spending enough. When the squire had overtaken them, they would not suffer him to ride with them, but sent him home again to comfort their mother, praying her meekly for her blessing.

So this squire was benighted as he rode homeward, and by misfortune happened to come into the castle of a baron whose brother (a false knight and betrayer of ladies and of good knights) Sir Aglovale had slain. When this baron knew from the squire that he served a good knight called Sir Aglovale, he commanded his men to have him away without mercy.

On the morn came Sir Aglovale and Sir Percivale riding by a churchyard where men and women were busy in burying this same dead squire. When the brothers heard from a good man of the company how the baron had shamefully slain the squire that night, they alighted both, left their horses with their men, and went on foot to the castle. All so soon as they were within the castle gate Sir Aglovale bade the porter "Go thou unto thy lord and tell him that I am Sir Aglovale, for whom the squire was slain this night."

Anon the lord of the castle, whose name was Goodewin, came armed into the court, and he and Sir Aglovale lashed together as eagerly as it had been two lions. Sir Percivale fought with all the remnant that would fight, and within a while had slain all that would withstand him, for he dealt so his strokes that there durst no man abide him. Within a while Sir Aglovale had Sir Goodewin also at the earth, and so the two brethren departed and took their horses. Then they let carry the dead squire unto a priory, and there they interred him. When this was done they rode their way into many countries, ever inquiring after Sir Launcelot, but never they could hear of him.

At last, at a castle that was called Cardican, Sir Percivale parted from Sir Aglovale, and with his squire rode alone. In the afternoon he came upon a bridge of stone, where he found a knight that was bound with a chain fast about unto a pillar of stone. This was Sir Persides, a knight of the Table Round, who by adventure came this way and lodged in the castle at the bridge foot. There by an evil custom of the castle men set upon him suddenly or ever he might come to his weapon, and bound him, and chained him at the bridge. There he knew he should die unless some man of honour brake his bands.

"Be ye of good cheer," said Sir Percivale, "and because ye are a knight of the Round Table as well as I, I trust to God to make you free."

Therewith Sir Percivale drew out his sword, and struck at the chain with such a might that he cut a-two the chain, and through Sir Persides' hauberk, and hurt him a little.

"Truly," said Sir Persides, "that was a mighty stroke if ever I felt one, for had it not been for the chain, ye had slain me."

Therewithal Sir Persides saw a knight coming out of the castle, flying all that ever he might. "Beware, sir," said he; "yonder cometh a man that will have ado with you."

"Let him come," said Sir Percivale.

So he met with that knight in the midst of the bridge, and gave him such a buffet that he smote him quite from his horse and over a part of the bridge so that, had there not been a little vessel under the bridge, that knight had been drowned. Then Sir Percivale took the knight's horse, and made Sir Persides to mount upon him. So they rode to the castle, and made the lady deliver Sir Persides' servants.

Had he not had a great matter in hand, he would have remained to do away with the evil customs there. But Sir Percivale might not long abide, for he rode to seek Sir Launcelot.

Sir Persides brought him unto his own castle, and there made him great cheer for that night. Then on the morn, when Sir Percivale had heard mass and broken his fast, he said to Sir Persides: "Ride unto King Arthur, and tell the King how that ye met with me, and tell my brother Sir Aglovale how I rescued you, and bid him seek not after me, for I am in the quest to seek Sir Launcelot of the Lake, and will not see him or the court till Sir Launcelot is found. Also tell Sir Kay and Sir Mordred that I trust to God to be of as good worthiness as either of them, and that I will never see that court till men speak more honour of me than ever men did of any of them both."

So Sir Persides departed from Sir Percivale, and rode unto King Arthur, and told there of Sir Percivale. And King Arthur said he must needs prove a good knight, for his father and his brethren were noble knights.

Now turn we to Sir Launcelot, and speak we of his care and woe and what pain he endured from cold, hunger, and thirst. As he wandered like a mad man here and there, he by fortune came to the castle of King Pelles. There he was healed of his madness, and when he was recovered he was sore ashamed that he had thus been clean out of his wit. And King Pelles gave him his castle of Bliant, that stood in an island enclosed with a fair water, deep and large. Sir Launcelot called it the Joyous Isle, and here he dwelt a long while. Because he was driven from King Arthur's court he desired not to be known, and he named himself "The knight that hath trespassed."

Now it fell at that time that Sir Launcelot heard of a jousting hard by his castle, and he sent word thither that there was one knight in the Joyous Isle, by name "The knight that hath trespassed," that will joust against any knights that will come to him. When this cry was made, unto Joyous Isle drew many knights, and wit you well there was not seen at Arthur's court one knight that did so much deeds of arms as were done in that gay castle.

And in the meanwhile came also Sir Percivale nigh to Joyous Isle, and would have gone to that castle, but might not for the broad water. Then he saw on the other side a lady, and he called unto her and asked who was in that castle.

"Fair knight," she said, "here within this castle is the fairest knight and the mightiest man that is, I dare say, living, and he calleth himself 'The knight that hath trespassed.' He came into this country like a mad man, with dogs and boys chasing him, and by miracle he was brought into his wit again. If ye list to come into the castle, ye must ride unto the farther side of the isle, and there ye shall find a vessel that will bear you and your horse."

Then Sir Percivale came unto the vessel, and passed the water. When he came to the castle gate, he bade the porter, "Go thou to the good knight within the castle, and tell him here is come an errant knight to joust with him."

Sir Percivale now rode within the castle, and anon Sir Launcelot had warning, he was soon ready. And there Sir Percivale and Sir Launcelot encountered with such a might that both the horses and the knights fell to the earth. Then they left their horses, swung out noble swords, and hewed away pieces of their shields, and dashed together like two boars, and either wounded other passing sore.

At the last Sir Percivale spake, when they had fought there more than two hours: "Fair knight," saith he, "I pray thee tell me thy name, for I met never with such a knight."

"Sir," said Sir Launcelot, "my name is 'The knight that hath trespassed.' Now tell me your name, I pray you, gentle knight."

"Truly," said Sir Percivale, "my name is Sir Percivale of Galis; King Pellinore was my father and Sir Aglovale is my brother."

"Alas," said Sir Launcelot, "what have I done to fight with you that art a knight of the Table Round, that sometime was your fellow."

Therewithal Sir Launcelot kneeled down upon his knees, and threw away his shield and his sword from him. When Sir Percivale saw him do so, he marvelled what he meant. Then he begged him upon the high order of knighthood to tell his true name, and Sir Launcelot told him all.

"Alas," said Sir Percivale, "what have I done! I was sent by the Queen for to seek you, and so I have sought you nigh these two years. I pray you forgive me mine offence that I have here done."

"It is soon forgiven," said Sir Launcelot.

Then Sir Percivale told him how King Arthur and all his knights, and in especial Queen Guenever, made great dole and sorrow that ever he departed from them, and that never knight was better welcome back to the court than he would be. So Sir Launcelot agreed to do after Sir Percivale's counsel, and ride with him to the King.

So then they took their horses and departed from the Joyous Isle, and within five days' journey they came to Camelot, that is called in English Winchester. And when Sir Launcelot was come among them, the King and all the knights made great joy of him. Then Sir Percivale of Galis began and told the whole adventures, and all the tales of Sir Launcelot. And the Queen made great cheer, and there were great feasts made, and many great lords and ladies, when they heard that Sir Launcelot was come to the court again, made great joy.

Of the Coming of Sir Galahad

At the vigil of Pentecost, when all the fellowship of the Round Table were come unto Camelot, and the tables were set ready to the meat, right so entered into the hall a full fair gentlewoman before the King, and on behalf of King Pelles requested that Sir Launcelot should go with her hereby into a forest. Sir Launcelot bade his squire saddle his horse and bring his arms, and right so he departed with the gentlewoman, and rode until that he came into a great valley, where they saw an abbey of nuns. There was a squire ready, and opened the gates; and so they entered and descended off their horses, and there came a fair fellowship about Sir Launcelot and welcomed him, and were passing glad of his coming.

In the meanwhile there came twelve nuns which brought with them Galahad, the which was passing fair and well made, so that in the world men might scarcely find his match. "Sir," said the ladies, "we bring you here this child, the which we have nourished, and we pray you to make him a knight; for of a worthier man's hand may he not receive the order of knighthood."

Sir Launcelot beheld that young squire, and saw him seemly and demure as a dove, with all manner of good features, and he thought of his age never to have seen so fair a man of form. Then said Sir Launcelot, "Cometh this desire of himself?"

He and all they said, "Yea."

"Then shall he," said Sir Launcelot, "receive the high order of knighthood to-morrow."

That night Sir Launcelot had passing good cheer, and on the morn at the hour of prime, at Galahad's desire, he made him knight, and said, "God make you a good man, for beauty faileth you not as any that liveth."

Then Sir Launcelot departed from them, and came again unto Camelot by the hour of nine on Whitsunday morning. By that time the King and the Queen and all the fellowship were gone to the minster to hear the service.

When they were come from service all were passing glad of Sir Launcelot's return. And as they entered the hall each of the barons sought his name, written with gold letters, in the sieges of the Round Table. Thus they went along from seat to seat, until that they came to the Siege

Perilous, where they found letters newly written of gold, that said: "Four hundred winters and fifty-four accomplished after the passion of our Lord Jesu Christ ought this siege to be filled."

All thought this a marvellous thing, and an adventurous. And then Sir Launcelot accounted the term of the writing from the birth of our Lord unto that day, and said: "It seemeth me this siege ought to be filled this same day, for this is the feast of Pentecost after the four hundred and four and fifty years; and if it would please all parties, I would none of these letters were seen this day, till he be come that ought to achieve this adventure."

Then they provided a cloth of silk for to cover these letters in the Siege Perilous, and the King bade haste unto dinner.

It was an old custom of Arthur's court that on this day they should not sit at their meat until they had seen some adventure. As they stood waiting therefor, in came a squire bringing the marvellous tidings that beneath at the river there was a great stone, as it were of red marble, floating above the water, wherein a sword stuck. So the King and all the knights went unto the river to see this marvel, and they found it even as the squire had said. There in the stone was the fair rich sword, and in the pommel thereof were precious stones and subtile letters wrought with gold. Then the barons read the letters, which said in this wise: "Never shall man take me hence but only he by whose side I ought to hang, and he shall be the best knight of the world."

When the King had seen these letters, he said unto Sir Launcelot, "Fair sir, this sword ought to be yours, for I am sure ye be the best knight of the world."

Then Sir Launcelot answered full soberly, conscious of a great sin: "Certes, sir, it is not my sword; also, sir, wit ye well I have no hardiness to set my hand thereto, for it belongs not by my side."

"Now, fair nephew," said the King unto Sir Gawaine, "assay ye to take the sword for my love."

Therewith Sir Gawaine took the sword by the handles, though unwillingly and only at the King's commandment, but he might not stir it. Then the King said unto Sir Percivale that he should assay. So he set his hand on the sword and drew it strongly, but he might not move it. Then were there more that durst be so hardy as to set their hands thereto, but all failed.

"Now may ye go to your dinner," said Sir Kay unto King Arthur, "for a marvellous adventure have ye seen."

So the King and all went in, and every knight knew his own place and set himself therein, and all sieges were filled save only the Siege Perilous. Anon there befell a marvellous adventure, for all the doors and the windows of the place shut of themselves, yet then the hall was not greatly darkened, and therewith they were amazed, both one and other.

While they sat there in suspense as to what should happen, came in a good old man, and an ancient, clothed all in white, and there was no knight knew from whence he came. With him he brought a young knight in red arms, without sword or shield, save a scabbard hanging by his side. Then the old man said unto Arthur, "Sir, I bring here a young knight the which is of king's lineage and of the kindred of Joseph of Arimathea, whereby the marvels of this court and of strange realms shall be fully accomplished."

The King was right glad of the good man's words, and bade him and the young knight welcome. Then the old man made the young man unarm; and he was in a coat of red silk, and bore a mantle upon his shoulder that was furred with ermine. Anon the old knight led him unto the Siege Perilous, where beside sat Sir Percivale and Sir Launcelot. The good man lifted up the cloth, and found there letters that said thus: "This is the siege of Galahad, the high prince." He set him down surely in that siege, saying, "Wit ye well that place is yours," and then, departed and went his way.

All the knights of the Table Round marvelled greatly that Sir Galahad durst sit there in that Siege Perilous, and was so tender of age; for never before had anyone sat therein but he was mischieved. And they foresaw that Sir Galahad would come to great honour, and outdo them all in knightly courtesy.

Then the King bade him welcome to the court, and taking him by the hand, went down from the palace to show Galahad the adventures of the stone. "Sir" said the King unto him, "here is a great marvel as ever I saw, and right good knights have assayed and failed."

"Sir," said Galahad, "that is no marvel, for this adventure is not theirs but mine, and for the surety of this sword I brought none with me; for here by my side hangeth the scabbard."

Anon he laid his hand on the sword, and lightly drew it out of the stone and put it in the sheath, saying, "Now it goeth better than it did aforehand."

How the Quest of the Holy Grail Was Begun

The dish from which our Lord Jesu Christ ate the paschal lamb at His last supper with His disciples men call the Holy Grail. Therein also Joseph of Arimathea caught the last drops of sacred blood, and after the passion of our Lord that gentle knight, the which took down the body off the holy cross, at that time departed from Jerusalem with a great party of his kindred, bearing the Holy Grail with them.

It befell that they came first to a city that was called Sarras, and at the last they crossed to Britain, and through them all the heathen people of this land were turned to the Christian faith.

Ever as years went by the Holy Grail became more precious, and the possession of it ever more a sacred trust. But after a long while it was lost from the world through men's sinfulness, and only those of pure heart and life might from time to time see it.

Merlin, before he was put under the stone, had foreseen that by them which should be fellows of the Round Table the truth of the Holy Grail would be well known, and in the good days of King Arthur the longing grew to be worthy of the vision of this sign of the Lord's presence among men. Moreover a holy hermit had said that, when the Siege Perilous was filled, the achieving of the Holy Grail should be near.

After Galahad drew the sword out of the stone the King and all estates went thoughtful home unto Camelot, and so to even-song in the great minster. After that they went to supper, and every knight sat in his own place at the Round Table. Then anon they heard cracking and crying of thunder that should, as it seemed to them, shake the place all to pieces. In the midst of this blast entered a sunbeam more clear by seven times than ever they saw day, and all they were alighted of the grace of the Holy Ghost.

Then began every knight to behold other, and either saw other by their seeming fairer than ever they looked afore. There was no knight might speak one word, and so they looked every man on his fellows, as if they were dumb. Then there entered into the hall the Holy Grail, covered with white samite, but there was none might see it, or who bare it. And there was all the hall filled full with good odours, and every knight was nourished in his soul. When the Holy Grail had been borne through the hall, then it departed suddenly, so that they wist not what became of it.

Then had they all breath to speak, and the King yielded thankings unto God for His good grace that He had sent them. "Now," said Sir Gawaine, "we have been richly blessed this day, but one thing beguiled us,—we might not see the Holy Grail, it was so preciously covered. Wherefore I will make here avow, that to-morn, without longer abiding, I shall labour in the quest of the Holy Grail a twelvemonth and a day, or more if need be, and shall not return unto the court till I have seen it more openly than it hath been seen here; and if I may not speed, I shall return again at the end of the time as he that may not be against the will of our Lord Jesu Christ."

When they of the Table Round heard Sir Gawaine say so, the most part of them arose, and made such avows as Sir Gawaine had made. Anon as King Arthur heard this he was greatly grieved, for he wist well that they might not gainsay their avows, and he should be bereft of the fairest fellowship and the truest knighthood that ever were seen together in any realm of the world. For, when they departed from hence, they should never all meet again in this world, and many of his true fellowship of noble knights should die in the quest.

When the Queen also and all the court wist these tidings, they had such sorrow and heaviness that there might no tongue tell it. Many of the ladies would have gone with the knights that they loved, had not an old man in religious clothing said on high that none in this quest should lead wife with him. Moreover he warned the knights plainly that he that was not clean of his sins should not see the mysteries of our Lord Jesu Christ. Then they went to rest themselves, and in honour of the highness of Galahad he was led into King Arthur's chamber, and there rested in his own bed.

As soon as it was day the King arose, for he had no rest all that night for sorrow. Then the King and the Queen went unto the minster, and all the knights, armed fully save their shields and their helms, followed them to hear the service.

Then after the service was done, the King would wit how many had taken the quest of the Holy Grail, and found by tale there were an hundred and fifty, all knights of the Round Table. Then they put on their helms, and so mounted upon their horses, and rode through the streets of

Camelot. And there was weeping of rich and poor, and the King turned away, and might not speak for weeping.

Within a while they came to a city and a castle called Vagon. The lord of that castle was a good old man and set open the gates, and made them all the good cheer that he might. On the morrow they were all accorded that they should ride every each from other. Then they departed with weeping and mourning cheer, and every knight took the way that him best liked.

How Galahad Gat Him a Shield

Now Sir Galahad was yet without shield, and so he rode four days without any adventure. After even-song of the fourth day he came to a white abbey, and there he was received with great reverence, and led to a chamber wherein he was ware of two knights of the Round Table, the one King Bagdemagus and the other Sir Uwaine. They went unto him and made of him great solace; and they told him that within this place was a shield that no man might bear about his neck without great harm to himself, unless he were the worthiest knight of the world.

[Illustration: Sir Galahad]

"Ah, sir," said King Bagdemagus to Galahad, "I shall to-morrow assay this strange adventure, and if I may not achieve it ye shall take it upon you, for I am sure ye shall not fail."

"Sir," said Galahad, "I agree right well thereto, for I have no shield."

So on the morn they arose and heard mass. Then King Bagdemagus asked where the adventurous shield was. Anon a monk led him behind an altar, where the shield hung as white as any snow, but in the midst was a red cross. The monk counselled him to be well advised before taking it, and King Bagdemagus answered:

"Well, I wot well that I am not the best knight of the world, but yet shall I assay to bear it."

And so, bidding Sir Galahad to abide there still, till it was known how he sped, King Bagdemagus bore the red cross shield out of the monastery, took with him a squire, the which should bring tidings unto Sir Galahad how he sped, and rode away.

Two miles off they came into a fair valley afore a hermitage, and there they saw a goodly knight in white armour, horse and all. He came as fast as his horse might run, with his spear in the rest, and King Bagdemagus dressed his spear against him, and brake it upon the White Knight. The other struck him so hard that he brake the mails, and thrust him through the right shoulder, for the shield covered him not at that time, and so he bare him from his horse.

Therewith the White Knight alighted and took the white shield from King Bagdemagus, saying, "Knight, thou hast done thyself great folly, for this shield ought not to be borne but by him that shall have no peer that liveth." Then he came to the squire, and said, "Bear this shield unto the good knight Sir Galahad, that thou left in the abbey, and greet him well from me."

The squire first went unto Bagdemagus, and asked him whether he were sore wounded or not. "Yea, forsooth," said he, "I shall escape hard from death." Then the squire fetched his horse, and brought him with great pain unto an abbey. Then was he taken down safely, and unarmed, and laid in a bed. There his wounds were looked to, and, as the book telleth, he lay there long, and escaped hard with life.

"Sir," said the squire, when he came to Galahad, "that knight that wounded Bagdemagus sendeth you greeting, and bade that ye should bear this shield, wherethrough great adventures should befall."

"Now blessed be God," said Sir Galahad. Then he asked his arms, mounted upon his horse, and, commending himself unto God, hung the white shield about his neck. So he departed, and within a while came by the hermitage, where the White Knight awaited him. Every each saluted other courteously, and the knight told Sir Galahad the marvels of the shield.

"Sir," said he, "at that same hour that Joseph of Arimathea came to Sarras, there was a king in that city called Evelake, that had great war against the Saracens, and there Joseph made this shield for him in the name of Him that died upon the cross. Then through his good belief he had the better of his enemies; for when King Evelake was in the battle, there was a cloth set afore the shield, and when he was in the greatest peril he let put away the cloth, and then his enemies saw a figure of a man on the cross, wherethrough they all were discomfited.

"Soon afterwards Joseph departed from Sarras, and King Evelake would go with him whether he would or nould, and they came unto this land of Britain. Not long after this, when Joseph lay on his death-bed, King Evelake begged of him some token that would lead him to think on the old knight for love of whom he had left his own country. So Joseph took this shield, and thereupon he made a cross with his own blood; that should be Evelake's token. Then he said that no man should bear this shield until the time that Galahad come, the last of Joseph's lineage, that should do many marvellous deeds while bearing it about his neck. To-day is the time they then set when ye shall have King Evelake's shield."

So spake the White Knight, and then vanished away; and Sir Galahad rode with the squire back to the abbey.

Sir Galahad at the Castle of Maidens

The men of the abbey made great joy of Sir Galahad, and he rested there that night. Upon the morn he gave the order of knighthood to the squire who had brought him the red-cross shield, and asked him his name, and of what kindred he was come.

"Sir," said he, "men call me Melias of Lile, and I am the son of the King of Denmark."

"Now, fair sir," said Galahad, "since ye are of noble birth, see that knighthood be well placed in you, for ye ought to be a mirror unto all chivalry."

"Sir," said Melias, "ye say truly. But, sir, since ye have made me a knight, ye must of right grant me my first desire that is reasonable."

"Ye say truly," said Galahad.

Then Melias said, "Suffer me to ride with you in this quest of the Holy Grail till some adventure part us."

"I grant you, sir," said Galahad.

Then men brought Sir Melias his armour and his spear and his horse; and so Sir Galahad and he rode forth all that week ere they found any adventure. And then upon a Monday, in the morning, as they had departed from an abbey, they came to a fork in the road, where stood written these words: "Now ye knights errant, who go to seek knights adventurous, see here two ways; the right-hand road ye are warned against, for knight shall never ride out of that place again unless he be a good man and a worthy knight; and if ye go to the left hand ye shall not there easily win prowess, for ye shall in this road be soon attacked."

"Sir," said Melias to Galahad, "if ye are pleased to suffer me to take the way on the left hand, tell me, for there I shall well prove my strength."

"It were better," said Galahad, "ye rode not that way, for I believe I should better escape in that way than ye."

"Nay, my lord," said Melias, "I pray you, let me have that adventure."

"Take it, in God's name," said Galahad.

So Melias rode far through an old forest, and after two days or more came into a fair meadow. Here in a fair lodge of boughs he espied a chair wherein was a subtilely-wrought crown of gold, and near by was a cloth spread upon the ground with many delicious meats upon it. Sir Melias had no desire for the food, but the crown of gold pleased him much, so he stooped down and took it and rode his way with it. And anon he saw a knight come riding after him, who called upon him to set down the crown that was not his, and to defend himself.

The new-made knight was glad of this adventure, and the two let their horses run as fast as they might, so that the other knight smote Sir Melias through his hauberk and through the left side, and he fell to the earth nigh dead. Then the knight took the crown and went his way, and Sir Melias lay still, and had no power to stir. In the meanwhile by good fortune there came Sir Galahad and found him there in peril of death.

Then he said, "Ah, Melias, who hath wounded you? It would have been better to ride the other way."

And when Sir Melias heard him speak, "Sir," he said, "for God's love let me not die in this forest, but bear me unto the abbey near at hand."

"It shall be done," said Galahad, "but where is he that hath wounded you?"

With that Sir Galahad heard some one cry, "Knight, keep thee from me!"

"Ah, sir," said Melias, "beware, for that is he that hath slain me."

Sir Galahad answered, "Sir knight, come at your peril."

So they came together as fast as their horses might run; and Galahad smote the other so that his spear went through the knight's shoulder and smote him down off his horse, and in the falling Galahad's spear brake. With that came out another knight from the leaves, and brake a spear upon Galahad before he might turn about. Then Galahad drew out his sword and smote this one so that he fled away, and Sir Galahad pursued fast after him. But soon he turned again unto Sir Melias, and there he alighted and placed him softly on his horse before him, and Sir Galahad climbed up behind, and held him in his arms, and so brought him to the abbey and into his chamber. Here he placed the wounded knight in the care of an old monk, that promised to heal him of his wounds.

"Now I will depart," said Galahad, "for I have much on hand; many good knights be full busy about it, and this knight and I were in the same quest of the Holy Grail."

"Sir," said the good monk, "for his sins he was thus wounded; and I marvel," said he to Melias, "how ye durst take upon you so rich a thing as the high order of knighthood without clean confession, and that was the cause ye were bitterly wounded. For the way on the right hand betokeneth the high way of our Lord Jesu Christ, and the way of a true good liver. And the other way betokeneth the way of sinners and of misbelievers. Your pride and presumption in taking the quest of the blessed Holy Grail made you to be overthrown, for it may not be achieved but by virtuous living. Pride is head of all deadly sins, and that caused you to depart from Sir Galahad. And when ye took the crown of gold your sin was covetousness and theft. But this Galahad, the holy knight, the which fought with the two knights that signify the two deadly sins which were wholly in you, was able to overthrow them, for he is pure in his heart."

"My lord Galahad," said Sir Melias, "as soon as I may ride I shall seek you."

"God send you health," said Galahad, and so he took his horse and departed, and rode many journeys forward and backward, as adventure would lead him.

Then Sir Galahad came unto a mountain. There he found an old chapel, where all was desolate, and he knelt before the altar and besought of God wholesome counsel. As he prayed, he heard a voice that said, "Go thou now, thou adventurous knight, to the Castle of Maidens, and there do thou away the wicked customs."

When Sir Galahad heard this, he thanked God and took his horse, and he had ridden but half a mile when he saw in a valley afore him a strong castle with deep ditches, and there ran beside it a fair river, that was called Severn. Then he met with a man of great age. Either saluted other, and Galahad asked him the castle's name. "Fair sir," said he, "it is the Castle of Maidens."

"That is a cursed castle," said Galahad, "and all who have intercourse therein are cursed, for all pity is lacking there, and all cruelty and mischief are therein."

"Therefore I counsel you, sir knight," said the other, "that ye turn back."

"Sir," said Sir Galahad, "ye may be sure I shall not turn back."

Then Sir Galahad looked on his armour to see that nothing was lacking, and he put his shield afore him, and anon there met him seven fair maidens, which said unto him, "Sir knight, ye ride here in great folly, for ye have the water to pass over."

"Why should I not pass the water?" said Galahad. So he rode away from them, and met with a squire, who said. "Knight, those knights in the castle defy you, and forbid you to go farther till they know what ye would."

"Fair sir," said Galahad, "I come to destroy the wicked customs of this castle."

"Sir," said the squire, "if ye will abide by that, ye shall have enough to do."

The squire entered into the castle, and anon there came out seven knights, all brethren. And when they saw Galahad they cried, "Knight, defend thyself, for we assure thee nothing but death."

Then Galahad put forth his spear, and smote the foremost to the earth. And therewith all the others smote him on his shield great strokes so that their spears brake. Then Sir Galahad drew out his sword, and set upon them so hard that it was marvel to see it, and so, through great force, he made them to forsake the field. Galahad chased them till they entered into the castle, and then passed through the castle and out at another gate.

Now there met Sir Galahad an old man, who said, "Sir, have here the keys of this castle."

Then Sir Galahad opened the gates, and saw so many people in the passages that he might not number them, and all said, "Sir, ye be welcome, for long have we awaited here our deliverance."

Then came to him a gentlewoman, and said, "These knights are fled, but they will come again this night, and here begin again their evil practices."

"What will ye that I shall do?" said Galahad.

"Sir," said the gentlewoman, "that ye send after all the knights hither that hold their lands of this castle, and make them to swear to use the customs that were used heretofore of old time."

"I will well," said Galahad.

She brought him a horn of ivory, richly bound with gold, and said, "Sir, blow this horn, which will be heard two miles about this castle."

When Sir Galahad had blown the horn he set himself down upon a bed. Then a priest came and told him of the evil practices of the castle, and why it was called the Castle of Maidens. "It chanced in this wise," said he: "More than seven years agone the seven brethren came, and lodged with the lord of this castle and of all the country round about. When they espied the duke's daughter, a full fair woman, they plotted falsely betwixt themselves and slew the duke and his eldest son. Then they took the maiden and the treasure of the castle, and by great force they held all the knights of this castle against their will under their power in great slavery, and robbed and pillaged the poor common people of all that they had. Then it happened on a day the duke's daughter said, 'Ye have done unto me great wrong to slay my own father and my brother, and thus to hold our lands. But ye shall not hold this castle many years, for by one knight ye shall be overcome.' Thus she had prophesied seven years agone.

"'Well,' said the seven knights, 'if that be so, there shall never lady nor knight pass by this castle but they shall abide here, whether they will or not, or die for it, till that knight be come by whom we shall lose this castle.' Therefore it is called the Maidens' Castle, for many maidens have here been destroyed."

By the time the priest had finished, the knights of the country were come at the call from the ivory horn. Then Sir Galahad made them do homage and fealty to the duke's daughter, and set the people in great ease of heart.

And the next morning one came to Galahad and told him how Gawaine, Gareth, and Uwaine had slain the seven brethren. "I am glad to hear it," said Sir Galahad, and he took his armour, mounted his horse, and commended the people of the Castle of Maidens unto God, and so rode away.

Sir Launcelot's Repentance

When Sir Galahad was departed from the Castle of Maidens, he rode till he came to a waste forest, and there he met with Sir Launcelot and Sir Percivale, but they knew him not, for he was new disguised. Right so, Sir Launcelot dressed his spear, and brake it upon Sir Galahad; and Sir Galahad smote him so again, that he smote down horse and man. Then he drew his sword, and dressed him unto Sir Percivale, and smote him so on the helm that, had not the sword swerved, Sir Percivale had been slain, and with the stroke he fell out of his saddle.

This joust was done tofore the hermitage where a recluse dwelt, and, when she saw Sir Galahad ride, she said, "God be with thee, best knight of the world. Ah, verily, if yonder two knights had known thee as well as I do, they would not have encountered with thee."

When Sir Galahad heard her say so, he was sore adread to be known. Therefore he smote his horse with his spurs, and rode at a great pace away from them. Then perceived they both that he was Galahad, and up they gat on their horses, and rode fast after him, but in a while he was out of their sight. Then they turned again with heavy cheer, and Sir Percivale said, "Let us ask some tidings at yonder recluse."

"Do as ye list," said Sir Launcelot. So Sir Percivale turned back, but Sir Launcelot rode on across and endlong in a wild forest, and held no path, but as wild adventure led him. At last he came to a stone cross, which pointed two ways, and by the cross was a stone that was of marble; but it was so dark that he might not wit what it was.

Sir Launcelot looked about him, and saw an old chapel. There he expected to find people, so he tied his horse, and took off his shield and hung it upon a tree. Then he went to the chapel door, and found it waste and broken. Within he saw a fair altar full richly arrayed with cloth of clean silk, and there stood a fair clean candlestick of silver which bare six great candles.

When Sir Launcelot saw this light, he had great will to enter into the chapel, but he could find no place where he might enter. Then was he passing heavy and dismayed. He returned to his horse, took off his saddle and bridle, and let him pasture. Then he unlaced his helm, and ungirded his sword, and laid himself down to sleep upon his shield tofore the cross.

[Illustration: Sir Launcelot at the Cross]

So he fell on sleep, and half waking and half sleeping he saw in a vision two fair white palfreys come toward him, bearing in a litter a sick knight. When he was nigh the cross he abode still, and Sir Launcelot heard him say, "Oh, sweet Lord, when shall this sorrow leave me? and when shall the holy vessel come by me, wherethrough I shall be blessed? For I have endured thus long for little trespass."

A full great while lamented the knight thus, and always Sir Launcelot heard it. Then he saw the candlestick with the six tapers come before the cross, yet he saw nobody that brought it. Also there came a table of silver, and the sacred vessel of the Holy Grail upon it.

Therewith the sick knight sat up, and, holding up both hands, he prayed that he might be whole of his malady. Then on his hands and knees he went so nigh that he touched the holy vessel, and kissed it, and anon he was whole. Then he said, "Lord God, I thank thee, for I am healed of this sickness."

When the holy vessel had been there a great while, it went unto the chapel, with the candlestick and the light, so that Launcelot wist not what became of it, for he was overtaken with a feeling of his sin, so that he had no power to arise and follow the holy vessel.

Then the sick knight raised himself up, and kissed the cross. Anon his squire brought him his arms, and asked his lord how he did. "Verily," said he, "I thank God, right well; through the holy vessel I am healed. But I have great marvel of this sleeping knight, that had no power to awake when the Holy Grail was brought hither."

"I dare right well say," said the squire, "that he dwelleth in some deadly sin, whereof he has never repented."

"By my faith," said the knight, "whatsoever he be, he is unhappy, for, as I deem, he is of the fellowship of the Round Table, the which is entered into the quest of the Holy Grail."

"Sir," said the squire, "here I have brought you all your arms, save your helm and your sword. By my assent now may ye take this knight's helm and his sword."

So he did, and when he was clean armed, he took Sir Launcelot's horse, for he was better than his own, and so they departed from the cross. Anon Sir Launcelot awoke, and bethought him what he had seen there, and whether it were a dream or not. Right so heard he a voice that said: "Sir Launcelot, more hard than is stone, more bitter than is wood, and more naked and barer than is the fig tree, go thou from hence, and withdraw thee from this holy place."

When Sir Launcelot heard this he was passing heavy, and wist not what to do. So he arose, sore weeping, and cursed the time when he was born, for he thought never to have honour more. Then he went to the cross, and found his helm, his sword, and his horse taken away. Then he called himself a very wretch, and the most unhappy of all knights. And he said: "My sin and my wickedness have brought me unto great dishonour. When I sought worldly adventures from worldly desires, I ever achieved them, and had the better in every place, and never was I discomfited in any quarrel, were it right or wrong. But now when I take upon me the adventures of holy things, I see and understand that mine old sin hindereth and shameth me, so that I had no power to stir or to speak when the Holy Grail appeared afore me."

Thus he sorrowed till it was day, and he heard the birds sing. Then somewhat he was comforted, but, when he missed his horse and his harness, he wist well God was displeased with him. He departed from the cross on foot into a forest, and came to a hermitage, and a hermit therein. There Launcelot kneeled down and cried on the Lord for mercy, and begged the hermit for charity to hear his confession.

"With a good will," said the good man; "art thou of King Arthur's court, and of the fellowship of the Round Table?"

"Yea, forsooth," was the answer, "and my name is Sir Launcelot of the Lake, that hath been right well said of; but now my good fortune is changed, for I am the worst wretch of the world."

The hermit beheld him, and had marvel how he was humbled.

"Sir," said he, "thou oughtest to thank God more than any knight living, for He hath caused thee to have more worldly honour than any other knight that now liveth. For thy presumption in taking upon thee, while in deadly sin, to be in His presence through the sacred vessel, that was the cause that thou mightest not see it with worldly eyes, for He will not appear where such sinners be, unless to their great hurt and shame. There is no knight living now that ought to give God so great thanks as thou; for He hath given thee beauty, seemliness, and great strength, above all other knights. Therefore thou art the more beholden unto God than any other man to love Him and fear Him; for thy strength and manhood will little avail thee if God be against thee."

Then Sir Launcelot wept with heavy cheer, for he knew the hermit said sooth.

"Sir," said the good man, "hide none old sin from me."

"Truly," said Sir Launcelot, "that were me full loath to disclose, for one thing that I have done I never disclosed these fourteen years, and for that may I now blame my shamelessness and my misadventure."

Then he told there that good man all his life, and how he had loved a queen unmeasurably, and out of measure long. "And," said he, "all my great deeds of arms that I have done, I did the most part for that queen's sake. For her sake would I battle, were it right or wrong; and never did I battle wholly for God's sake, but for to win honour and to make myself better beloved, and little or naught I thanked God for it. I pray you counsel me."

"I will counsel thee," said the hermit, "if thou wilt assure me that thou wilt never come into that queen's companionship when thou canst prevent it." This Sir Launcelot solemnly promised, whereupon the good man said, "Look that thy heart and mouth accord, and I assure thee that thou shalt have more honour than ever thou hadst. For it seemeth well God loveth thee, and in all the world men shall not find one knight to whom He hath given so much grace as He hath given thee; He hath given thee beauty with seemliness; He hath given thee wit, discretion to know good from evil; He hath given thee prowess and hardiness; and He hath given thee to work so largely that thou hast had at all times the better wheresoever thou camest. And now our Lord will suffer thee no longer, but that thou shalt know Him, whether thou wilt or nilt.

"Why the voice called thee bitterer than wood was because, where overmuch sin dwelleth, there may be but little sweetness; wherefore thou art likened to an old rotten tree. Why thou art harder than stone is because thou wilt not leave thy sin for any goodness that God hath sent thee; therefore thou art more than any stone, and never wouldest thou be made soft, neither by water nor by fire,—that is, the heat of the Holy Ghost may not enter in thee.

"Now shall I show thee why thou art more naked and barer than the fig tree. It befell that our Lord on Palm Sunday preached in Jerusalem, and there He found in the people that all hardness was harboured in them, and there He found in all the town not one that would harbour Him. And then He went without the town, and found in the midst of the way a fig tree, the which was right fair and well garnished of leaves, but fruit had it none. Then our Lord cursed the tree that bare no fruit; that likeneth the fig tree unto Jerusalem, that had leaves and no fruit. So thou, Sir Launcelot, when the Holy Grail was brought afore thee, He found in thee no fruit, nor good thought, nor good will, and thou wert befouled with sin."

"Verily," said Sir Launcelot, "all that ye have said is true, and from henceforward I undertake by the grace of God never to be so wicked as I have been, but to follow knighthood and to do feats of arms."

Then the good man enjoined Sir Launcelot to such penance as he might do, and to sue knighthood, and so blessed him, and prayed him to abide there all that day. "I will well," said Sir Launcelot, "for I have neither helm, nor horse, nor sword."

"As for that," said the good man, "I shall help you ere to-morn to a horse and all that belongeth unto you." And so Sir Launcelot repented him greatly.

Sir Percivale's Temptation

When Sir Percivale departed from the recluse to seek Sir Galahad, he rode till the hour of noon, when he met in a valley about twenty men of arms. As they saw him they asked him whence he was, and he answered, "Of the court of King Arthur." Then they cried all at once, "Slay him." Then Sir Percivale smote the first to the earth, and his horse upon him. Thereupon seven of the knights smote upon his shield all at once, and the remnant slew his horse, so that he fell to the earth.

So had they slain him or taken him, had not the good knight Sir Galahad, with the red arms, come there by adventure into those parts. And when he saw all those knights upon one knight, he cried, "Save me that knight's life." Then he dressed him towards the twenty men of arms as fast as his horse might drive, with his spear in the rest, and smote the foremost horse and man to the earth. And when his spear was broken he set his hand to his sword, and smote on the right hand and on the left hand, that it was marvel to see. At every stroke he smote one down, or put him to rebuke, so that they would fight no more, but fled to a thick forest, and Sir Galahad followed them.

When Sir Percivale saw him chase them so, he made great sorrow that his horse was away, for he wist well it was Sir Galahad. Then he cried aloud, "Ah, fair knight, abide and suffer me to do thankings unto thee, for much have ye done for me!"

But ever Sir Galahad rode so fast, that at the last he passed out of his sight, and Sir Percivale went after him on foot as fast as he might. Soon he met a yeoman riding upon a hackney, who led in his hand a great black steed, blacker than any bear.

"Ah, fair friend," said Sir Percivale, "as ever I may do for you and be your true knight in the first place ye will require me, I beg ye will lend me that black steed, that I may overtake a knight, the which rideth afore me."

"Sir knight," said the yeoman, "I pray you hold me excused of that, for that I may not do; for wit ye well, the horse belongs to a man that, if I lent it you or any other man, would slay me."

"Alas," said Sir Percivale, "I had never so great sorrow as I have for losing of yonder knight."

"Sir," said the yeoman, "I am right heavy for you, for a good horse would beseem you well, but I dare not deliver you this horse unless ye take it from me."

"That will I not do," said Sir Percivale.

So they departed, and Sir Percivale sat him down under a tree, and made sorrow out of measure. Anon the yeoman came pricking after as fast as ever he might, and asked Sir Percivale, "Saw ye, sir, any knight riding on my black steed? It hath been taken from me by force, wherefore my lord will slay me in what place he findeth me."

"Well," said Sir Percivale, "what wouldest thou that I did? Thou seest well that I am on foot, but had I a good horse I should bring him soon again."

"Sir," said the yeoman, "take my hackney and do the best ye can, and I shall follow you on foot, to wit how that ye shall speed."

Then Sir Percivale mounted upon that hackney, and rode as fast as he might. At the last he saw the knight on the black steed, and cried out to him to turn again. And he turned, and set his spear against Sir Percivale; and he smote the hackney in the midst of the breast, that he fell down dead to the earth. There Sir Percivale had a great fall, and the other rode his way.

Sir Percivale was very wroth, and cried, "Abide, wicked knight, coward and false-hearted knight, turn again and fight with me on foot."

He answered not, but passed on his way. When Sir Percivale saw he would not turn, he cast away his helm and sword, and thought himself unhappy above all other knights.

In this sorrow he abode all that day till it was night. Then he was faint, and laid him down and slept till it was midnight. Then he awaked, and saw afore him a woman which said unto him right fiercely, "Sir Percivale, abide here, and I shall go fetch you a horse, which shall bear you whither you will."

So she came soon again, and brought a horse with her that was inky black. When Sir Percivale beheld that horse, he marvelled that it was so great and so well apparelled. Courageously he leaped upon him, and took no heed of himself. As soon as ever he was mounted he thrust in the spurs, and so rode away by the forest, and the moon shone clear.

Within an hour, and less, the black steed bare him four day's journey thence, till he came to a rough water the which roared, and his horse would have borne him into it. And when Sir Percivale came nigh the brim, and saw the water so boisterous, he feared to overpass it. Then he made a sign of the cross in his forehead, whereupon the horse shook off Sir Percivale, and he fell into the water, crying and roaring, making great sorrow; and it seemed unto him that the water burned. Then Sir Percivale perceived the steed was a fiend, the which would have brought him unto his perdition. Then he commended himself unto God, and prayed our Lord to keep him from all such temptations.

So he prayed all that night till it was day. Then he saw that he was in a wild mountain the which was closed with the sea nigh all about, so that he might see no land about him which might relieve him. Then was Sir Percivale ware in the sea, and saw a ship come sailing towards him; and he went unto the ship, and found it covered within and without with white samite. At the board stood an old man clothed in a surplice in likeness of a priest.

"Sir," said Sir Percivale, "ye be welcome."

"God keep you," said the good man, "of whence be ye?"

"Sir," said Sir Percivale, "I am of King Arthur's court, and a knight of the Table Round, the which am in the quest of the Holy Grail. Here I am in great duress, and never likely to escape out of this wilderness."

"Doubt not," said the good man, "if ye be so true a knight as the order of chivalry requireth, and of heart as ye ought to be, ye need not fear that any enemy shall slay you."

"What are ye?" said Sir Percivale.

"Sir," said the old man, "I am of a strange country, and hither I come to comfort you, and to warn you of your great battle that shall befall you."

"With whom," said Sir Percivale, "shall I fight?"

"With the most champion of the world," said the old man, "but, if ye quit you well, ye shall lose no limb, even though vanquished and seemingly shamed to the world's end."

Then the good man leaped over the board, and the ship and all went away, Sir Percivale wist not whither. He abode there till midday, when he saw a ship come rowing in the sea as if all the winds of the world had driven it. It drove under the rock on which he sat; and when he hied thither he found the ship covered with silk blacker than any bier, and therein was a gentlewoman of great beauty, and she was clothed richly that none might be better.

When she saw Sir Percivale, she said, "Who brought you in this wilderness where ye be never like to pass hence? for ye shall die here for hunger and mischief."

"Damsel," said Sir Percivale, "I serve the best man of the world, and in His service He will not suffer me to die, for who that knocketh shall enter, and who that asketh shall have, and from the man that seeketh Him, He hideth Him not."

"And I came out of the waste forest where I found the red knight with the white shield," said the damsel.

"Ah, damsel," said he, "with that knight would I meet passing fain."

"Sir," said she, "if ye will ensure me, by the faith that ye owe unto knighthood, that ye will do my will what time I summon you, I shall bring you unto that knight."

"Yea," said he, "I shall promise you to fulfil your desire. But what are ye that proffereth me thus great kindness?"

"I am," said she, "a gentlewoman that am disherited, which was sometime the richest woman of the world."

"Damsel," said Sir Percivale, "who hath disherited you? for I have great pity of you."

"Sir," said she, "I dwell with the greatest man of the world, and he made me so fair and so clear that there was none like me, and of that great beauty I had a little pride, more than I ought to have had. Also I said a word that pleased him not, and then he would not suffer me to be any longer in his company. He drove me from mine heritage, and so disowned me, and he had never pity for me, and would none of my council nor of my court. Since, sir knight, it hath befallen me so, I and mine have taken from him many of his men, and have made them to become my men, for they ask never anything of me, but I give it them, that and much more. Therefore I and my servants war against him night and day. I know now no good knight and no good man but I get on my side, if I may. And since I know that ye are a good knight I beseech you to help me; and since ye are a fellow of the Round Table, ye ought not to fail any gentlewoman which is disherited, if she beseech you of help."

Then Sir Percivale promised her all the help that he might. She thanked him, and since the weather was at that time hot, she bade a gentlewoman bring a pavilion. So she did, and pitched it there upon the gravel. He slept a great while there in the heat of the day; and when he awoke, there was set before him upon a table all manner of meats that he could think of. Also he drank there the strongest wine that ever he drank, him thought, and therewith he was a little heated more than he ought to be. With that he beheld the gentlewoman, and him thought that she was the fairest creature that ever he saw.

When she saw him well refreshed, then she said, "Sir Percivale, wit ye well, I shall not fulfil your will, but if ye swear from henceforth to be my true servant, and do nothing but that I shall command you. Will ye ensure me this as ye be a true knight?"

Sir Percivale was on the point of promising her all, when by adventure and grace he saw his sword lie upon the ground, all naked, in whose pommel was a red cross. Then he bethought him of his knighthood and the warning spoken toforehand by the good man, and he made the sign of the cross in his forehead. Thereupon the pavilion turned up-so-down, and changed unto a smoke and a black cloud.

Sir Percivale was adread at this, and cried aloud, "Fair sweet Father, Jesu Christ, let me not be shamed, that was nigh lost, had not Thy good grace been!"

Then he looked upon the ship, and saw the damsel enter therein, which said, "Sir Percivale, ye have betrayed me." So she went with the wind roaring and yelling, that it seemed that all the water burned after her.

Then Sir Percivale made great sorrow, and drew his sword unto him saying, "Since my flesh will be my master, I shall punish it." Therewith he stabbed himself through the thigh so that the blood started, and he said, "O good Lord, take this in recompensation of that I have done against Thee, my Lord." Then he clothed him and armed him, and called himself a wretch, saying, "How nigh was I lost, and to have lost that I should never have gotten again, my honour as a pure man and worthy knight, for that may never be recovered after it is once lost."

As he thus made his moan, he saw the same ship come from the Orient that the good man was in the day before, and the noble knight was ashamed with himself, and therewith he fell in a swoon. When he awoke he went unto this good man weakly, and saluted him. Then he asked Sir Percivale, "How hast thou done since I departed?"

"Sir," said he, "here was a gentlewoman that led me into deadly sin," and there he told him all his temptation.

"Knew ye not the maid?" said the good man.

"Sir," said he, "nay; but well I wot the fiend sent her hither to shame me."

"Oh, good knight," said he, "that gentlewoman was the master fiend of hell, the champion that thou foughtest withal, the which would have overcome thee, had it not been for the grace of God. Now, beware, Sir Percivale, and take this for an ensample."

Then the good man vanished away, and Sir Percivale took his arms, and entered into the ship and so departed from thence.

The Victory of Sir Bors over Himself

When Sir Bors was departed from Vagon, he met with a religious man riding on an ass, and Sir Bors saluted him. Anon the good man knew him to be one of the knights errant that was in the quest of the Holy Grail.

"What are ye?" said the good man.

"Sir," said he, "I am a knight that fain would be counselled in the quest of the Holy Grail, for he shall have much earthly honour that may bring it to an end."

"Verily," said the good man, "that is sooth, for he shall be the best knight of the world, and the fairest of all the fellowship. But wit ye well, there shall none attain it but by cleanness of heart and of life."

So rode they together till they came to a hermitage, and there he prayed Bors to dwell all that night with him. So he alighted and put away his armour, and prayed him that he might be confessed. So they went into the chapel, and there he was clean confessed; and they ate bread and drank water together.

"Now," said the good man, "I pray thee that thou eat none other, till that thou sit at the table where the Holy Grail shall be."

"Sir," said he, "I agree thereto; but how wit ye that I shall sit there?"

"Yes," said the good man, "that know I, but there shall be few of your fellowship with you."

"All is welcome," said Sir Bors, "that God sendeth me."

Also the good man in sign of chastisement put on him a scarlet coat, instead of his shirt, and found him in so vigorous a life, and so stable, that he marvelled, and felt that he was never corrupt in fleshly lusts. Then Sir Bors put on his armour, and took his leave, and so departed.

After he had ridden a day or two on his road, he met about the hour of noon at the parting of two ways two knights, that led Lionel, his brother, bound upon a strong hackney and his hands bound tofore his breast. Each of the two held in his hands thorns, wherewith they went beating him so sore that the blood trailed down more than in a hundred places of his body. But he said never a word, as he which was great of heart; he suffered all that ever they did to him as though he had felt none anguish.

Anon Sir Bors dressed him to rescue him that was his brother. Just then he chanced to look upon his other side, and saw a knight which brought a fair gentlewoman, and would have dragged her into the thickest part of the forest out of the way of them that sought to rescue her.

Anon she espied where Sir Bors came riding. She deemed him a knight of the Round Table, wherefore she hoped to have some comfort; and she conjured him by the faith that he owed unto him in whose service he had entered, and the fidelity he owed unto the high order of knighthood, and for the noble King Arthur's sake, to help her in her sore distress.

When Sir Bors heard her cry, he had so much sorrow he knew not what to do. "For," said he, "if I let my brother be in adventure he must be slain, and that would I not for all the earth. And if I help not the maid in her peril, I am shamed for ever." Then he lifted up his eyes, and said weeping, "Fair Lord Jesu Christ, whose liege man I am, keep Lionel my brother, that these knights slay him not; and for Mary's sake, I shall succour this maid."

Then dressed he him unto the knight the which had the gentlewoman, and cried, "Sir knight, let your hand off that maiden, or ye be but a dead man."

The knight set down the maiden, and drew out his sword, but Bors smote him so hard that he beat him down to the earth. Then came twelve knights seeking the gentlewoman, and anon she told them all how Bors had delivered her. They made great joy, and besought him to come to her father, a noble lord; but Bors had a great adventure in hand, and might not delay. So he commended them unto God, and departed.

Then Sir Bors rode after Lionel his brother by the trace of their horses. He sought a great while; and at the last he overtook a man clothed in religious clothing, that told him Lionel was dead, and showed him a slain body, lying in a thicket, that well seemed to him the body of Lionel. Then he made such a sorrow that he fell to the earth all in a swoon, and lay a great while there.

When he came to himself he said, "Fair brother, since the company of you and me is parted, shall I never have joy in my heart; and now He which I have taken as to my Master, He be my help."

When he had said thus, he took the body lightly in his arms and put it upon the bow of his saddle, and so rode to an old feeble chapel fast by, and put him into a tomb of marble.

Then went Sir Bors from thence, and rode all that day, and then turned to a hermitage, at the entry of a forest. There he found Lionel his brother, which sat all armed at the chapel door. For he was yet on life, and a fiend had deceived Bors with the body left in the chapel, for to put him in error so that he might not find the blessed adventure of the Holy Grail.

When Sir Bors saw his brother alive he had great joy of him, that it was marvel to tell of his joy. And then he alighted off his horse, and said, "Fair sweet brother, when came ye thither?"

Anon as Sir Lionel saw him he said, "Ah, Bors, ye may make no boast. For all you I might have been slain. When ye saw two knights leading me away, beating me, ye left me for to succour a gentlewoman, and suffered me to remain in peril of death. Never before did any brother to another so great an untruth. And for that misdeed now I ensure you but death, for well have ye deserved it. Therefore guard yourself from henceforward, and that shall ye find needful as soon as I am armed."

When Sir Bors understood his brother's wrath, he kneeled down to the earth and cried him mercy, holding up both his hands, and prayed him to forgive him his evil will; but Lionel would show no pity, and made his avow to God that he should have only death. Right so he went in and put on his harness; then he mounted upon his horse and came tofore him, and said, "Bors, keep thee from me, for I shall do to thee as I would to a felon or a traitor, for ye be the untruest knight that ever came out of so worthy a house as was that of our father, King Bors of Ganis."

When Sir Bors saw that he must fight with his brother or else die, he wist not what to do. Then his heart counselled him not to fight, inasmuch as Lionel was born before him, wherefore he ought to bear him reverence. Again kneeled he down afore Lionel's horse's feet, and said, "Fair sweet brother, have mercy upon me and slay me not, and have in remembrance the great love which ought to be between us twain."

What Sir Bors said Lionel recked not, for the fiend had brought him in such a will that he was determined to slay him. Then when Lionel saw he would none other, and that he would not rise to give him battle, he rushed over him, so that his horse's feet smote Bors to the earth, and hurt him so sore that he swooned of distress. When Lionel saw this, he alighted from his horse to smite off his head. So he took him by the helm, and would have rent it from his head, had not the hermit come running unto him, which was a good man and of great age. Well had he heard all the words that were between them, and so fell down upon Sir Bors.

Then he said to Lionel, "Ah, gentle knight, have mercy upon me and on thy brother, for if thou slay him thou shalt commit a deadly sin, and that were sorrowful; for he is one of the worthiest knights of the world, and of the best conditions."

"So God me help," said Lionel, "sir priest, unless ye flee from him I shall slay you, and he shall never the sooner be quit."

"Verily," said the good man, "I had rather ye slay me than him, for my death shall not be great harm, not half so much as his."

"Well," said Lionel, "I am agreed"; and he set his hand to his sword, and smote the hermit so hard that his head went backward.

For all that, he restrained him not of his evil will, but took his brother by the helm, and unlaced it to strike off his head. And he would have slain him without fail, but so it happened that Colgrevance, a fellow of the Round Table, came at that time thither, as our Lord's will was. First he saw the good man slain, then he beheld how Lionel would slay his brother, whom he knew and loved right well. Anon he sprang down and took Lionel by the shoulders, and drew him strongly back from Bors, and said, "Lionel, will ye slay your brother, one of the worthiest knights of the world? That should no good man suffer."

"Why," said Sir Lionel, "will ye hinder me? If ye interfere in this, I shall slay you, and him after."

Then Lionel ran upon Bors, and would have smitten him through the head, but Sir Colgrevance ran betwixt them, and said, "If ye be so hardy as to do so more, we two shall meddle together."

Then Lionel defied him, and gave a great stroke through the helm. Now Colgrevance drew his sword, for he was a passing good knight, and defended himself right manfully. So long endured the battle that Sir Bors awoke from his swoon, and rose up all anguishly, and beheld Sir Colgrevance, the good knight, fight with his brother for his quarrel. Then was he full sorry and heavy, and would have risen to part them. But he had not so much might as to stand on foot, and must abide so long till Colgrevance had the worse, for Sir Lionel was of great chivalry and right hardy.

Only death awaited Colgrevance, when he beheld Sir Bors assaying to rise, and he cried, "Ah, Bors, come ye and cast me out of peril of death, wherein I have put me to succour you, which were right now nigh to death."

When Bors heard that, he did so much as to rise and put on his helm, making a marvellous sorrow at the sight of the dead hermit hard by. With that Lionel smote Colgrevance so sore that he bare him to the earth.

When he had slain Colgrevance, he ran upon his brother as a fiendly man, and gave him such a stroke that he made him stoop; and he, full of humility, prayed him for God's love to leave this battle. But Lionel would not, and then Bors drew his sword, all weeping, and said, "Fair brother, God knoweth mine intent. Ah, brother, ye have done full evil this day to slay such a holy priest, the which never trespassed. Also ye have slain a gentle knight, one of our fellows. And well wot ye that I am not afraid of you greatly, but I dread the wrath of God. This is an unkindly war; therefore may God show miracle upon us both. Now God have mercy upon me, though I defend my life against my brother."

With that Bors lifted up his hands, and would have smitten Lionel, but even then he heard a voice that said, "Flee, Bors, and touch him not."

Right so came a cloud betwixt them in likeness of a fire, so that both their shields burned. Then were they sore afraid, and fell both to the earth, and lay there a great while in a swoon. When they came to themselves, Bors saw that his brother had no harm, wherefore he gave thanks, for he feared God had taken vengeance upon him. With that he heard a voice say, "Bors, go hence and bear thy brother no longer fellowship, but take thy way anon right to the sea, for Sir Percivale abideth thee there."

So Sir Bors departed from Lionel, and rode the next way to the sea. On the strand he found a ship covered all with white samite. He alighted from his horse and entered into the ship, and anon it departed into the sea, and went so fast that him seemed the ship went flying. Then he saw in the midst of the ship a knight lie, all armed save his helm, and he knew that it was Sir Percivale. And either made great joy of other, that it was marvel to hear.

Then Sir Bors told Sir Percivale how he came into the ship, and by whose admonishment, and either told other of his temptations, as ye have heard toforehand. So went they downward in the sea, one while backward, another while forward, and each comforted other, and oft were they in their prayers. Then said Sir Percivale, "We lack nothing but Galahad, the good knight."

How Sir Launcelot Found the Holy Grail

When the hermit had kept Sir Launcelot three days, he gat him a horse, a helm, and a sword. So he departed, and took the adventure that God would send him. On a night, as he slept, there came a vision unto him, and a voice said, "Launcelot, arise up, and take thine armour, and enter into the first ship that thou shalt find."

When he heard these words, he started up and saw great clearness about him. Then he lifted up his hand in worship, and so took his arms, and made him ready. By adventure he came by a strand, and found a ship, the which was without sail or oar. And as soon as he was within the ship, he felt the most sweetness that ever he felt, and he was filled with a peace such as he had never known before. In this joy he laid himself down on the ship's board, and slept till day.

So Sir Launcelot was a month and more on the ship, and if ye would ask how he lived, as God fed the people of Israel with manna in the desert, so was he fed. On a night he went to play him by the waterside, for he was somewhat weary of the ship. And then he listened, and heard a horse come, and one riding upon him. When he came nigh he seemed a knight, and soon he saw that it was Galahad. And there was great joy between them, for there is no tongue can tell the joy that they made either of other; and there was many a friendly word spoken between them, the which need not here be rehearsed. And there each told other of the adventures and marvels that were befallen to them in many journeys since they were departed from the court.

So dwelled Launcelot and Galahad within that ship half a year, and served God daily and nightly with all their power. And often they arrived in isles far from folk, where there repaired none but wild beasts. There they found many strange adventures and perilous, which they brought to an end. But because the adventures were with wild beasts, and not in the quest of the Holy Grail, therefore the tale maketh here no mention thereof, for it would be too long to tell of all those adventures that befell them.

Thereafter it befell that they arrived in the edge of a forest tofore a cross, and then saw they a knight, armed all in white and richly horsed, leading in his right hand a white horse. He came to the ship and saluted the two knights on the high Lord's behalf, and said, "Galahad, sir, ye have been long enough with Launcelot. Come out of the ship, and start upon this horse, and go where the adventures shall lead thee in the quest of the Holy Grail."

So Galahad took sorrowful leave of Sir Launcelot, for they knew that one should never see the other before the dreadful day of doom. Galahad took his horse and entered into the forest, and the wind arose and drove Launcelot more than a month throughout the sea, where he slept little, but prayed to God that he might see some tidings of the Holy Grail.

And it befell on a night, at midnight, he arrived afore a castle, on the back side, which was rich and fair. There was a postern opened towards the sea, and was open without any keeping, save two lions kept the entry; and the moon shone clear. Anon Sir Launcelot heard a voice that said, "Launcelot, go out of this ship, and enter into the castle, where thou shalt see a great part of thy desire."

Then he ran for his arms, and so he went to the gate, and saw the lions. He set his hand to his sword, and drew it, whereupon there came a dwarf suddenly, and smote him on the arm so sore that the sword fell out of his hand. Then heard he a voice say, "Oh, man of evil faith and poor belief, wherefore trowest thou more on thy harness than in thy Maker? He in whose service thou art set might more avail thee than thine armour."

Then said Launcelot, "Fair Father Jesu Christ, I thank thee of Thy great mercy, that Thou reprovest me of my misdeed. Now see I well that ye hold me for your servant."

Then took he again his sword, and put it up in his sheath, and came to the lions, and they made semblant[1] to do him harm. Notwithstanding he passed by them without hurt, and entered into the castle to the chief fortress, and there were all at rest. Launcelot entered in so armed, for he found no gate nor door but it was open. At last he found a chamber whereof the door was shut, and he set his hand thereto to open it, but he might not, though he enforced himself much to undo the door.

Then he listened, and heard a voice which sang so sweetly that it seemed none earthly thing. Launcelot kneeled down tofore the chamber, for well wist he that there was the Holy Grail within that chamber. Then said he:

"Fair sweet Father Jesu Christ, if ever I did thing that pleased Thee, for Thy pity have me not in despite for my sins done aforetime, and show me something of that I seek!"

With that he saw the chamber door open, and there came out a great clearness, so that the house was as bright as if all the torches of the world had been there. So came he to the chamber door, and would have entered, but anon a voice said to him, "Flee, Launcelot, and enter not, for thou oughtest not to do it; and if thou enter thou shalt repent it."

He withdrew himself back right heavy, and then looked he up in the midst of the chamber, and saw a table of silver, and the holy vessel covered with red samite, and many angels about it. Right so came he to the door at a great pace, entered into the chamber, and drew towards the table of silver.

When he came nigh he felt a breath that seemed intermingled with fire, which smote him so sore in the visage that he thought it burned his visage. Therewith he fell to the earth, and had no power to arise. Then felt he many hands about him, which took him up and bare him out of the chamber door, and left him there seeming dead to all people.

Upon the morrow, when it was fair day, they within were arisen, and found Launcelot lying afore the chamber door, and all they marvelled how he came in. They looked upon him, and felt his pulse, to wit whether there were any life in him. And so they found life in him, but he might neither stand nor stir any limb that he had. They took him up, and bare him into a chamber, and laid him in a rich bed, far from all folk, and so he lay still as a dead man four and twenty days, in punishment, he afterwards thought, for the twenty-four years that he had been a sinner.

At the twenty-fifth day it befell that he opened his eyes, and the folk asked how it stood with him. He answered that he was whole of body, and then he would know where he was. They told him he was in the castle of Carboneck, and that the quest of the Holy Grail had been achieved by him, and that he should never see the sacred vessel more nearly than he had seen it.

Soon Sir Launcelot took his leave of all the fellowship that were there at the castle, and thanked them for the great labour. So he took his armour and departed, and said that he would go back to the realm of Logris.

[1] Made semblant: threatened.

The End of the Quest

Now, saith the story, Sir Galahad rode into a vast forest, wherein he rode many journeys, and he found many adventures, the which he brought to an end, whereof the story maketh here no mention. And on a day it befell him that he was benighted in a hermitage. The good man there was glad when he saw a knight-errant, and made him what cheer he might. Then when they were at rest, there came a gentlewoman knocking at the door, and called Galahad. So the hermit came to the door to wit what she would, and she said to him that she would speak with the knight that was lodged there. The good man awoke Galahad, and bade him arise and speak with a gentlewoman that seemed to have great need of him.

Then Galahad went to her, and asked her what she would. "Galahad," said she, "I will that ye arm you, and mount upon your horse and follow me, for I shall show you within these three days the highest adventure that ever any knight saw." Anon Galahad armed him, and took his horse, and bade the gentlewoman go, and he would follow as she liked.

So she rode as fast as her palfrey might bear her, till they came to the seaside, and there they found the ship wherein were Bors and Percivale, the which cried on the ship's board, "Sir Galahad, ye be welcome; we have awaited you long."

So, leaving his horse behind, Galahad entered into the ship, where the two knights received him with great joy. And the wind arose, and drove them through the sea marvellously.

Now saith the story that they rode a great while till they came to the castle of Carboneck, where Sir Launcelot had been tofore. They entered within the castle, and then there was great joy, for they wist well that they had fulfilled the quest of the Holy Grail.

As they were alone in the hall, it seemed to them that there came a man, in likeness of a bishop, with four angels from heaven, and held mass about a table of silver, whereupon the Holy Grail was. And in a vision they saw in the bread of the sacrament a figure in likeness of a child, and the visage was as bright as any fire.

Then said the bishop to them, "Servants of Jesu Christ, ye shall be fed afore this table with sweet food, that never knights tasted."

When he had said, he vanished away; and they sat them at the table in great reverence, and made their prayers. Then looked they, and saw a man that had all the signs of the passion of Jesu Christ, and he said: "My knights and my servants and my true children, which be come out of deadly life into spiritual life, I will now no longer hide me from you, but ye shall see now a part of my secrets and of my hid things; now hold and receive the high meat which ye have so much desired."

Then took He Himself the holy vessel, and came to Galahad, who knelt down and there he received the sacrament, and after him so received all his fellows; and they thought it so sweet that it was marvellous to tell.

Then said He to Galahad, "Son, knowest thou what I hold betwixt my hands?"

"Nay," said he, "unless ye will tell me."

"This is," said He, "the holy dish wherein I ate the lamb at the Last Supper. And now hast thou seen that thou most desiredst to see, but yet hast thou not seen it so openly as thou shalt see it in the city of Sarras, in the spiritual place. Therefore thou must go hence, and bear with thee this holy vessel, for this night it shall depart from the realm of Logris, that it shall never be seen more here. And knowest thou wherefore? Because they of this land be turned to evil living; therefore I shall disinherit them of the honour which I have done them. Therefore go ye three unto the sea, where ye shall find your ship ready."

Right so departed Galahad, Percivale and Bors with him. They rode three days, and then they came to a rivage[1], where they found the ship whereof the tale speaketh tofore. When they came to the board, they found in the midst the table of silver, which they had left in the castle of Carboneck, and the Holy Grail, which was covered with red samite. Then were they glad to have such things in their fellowship.

They had remained some time in the ship, when they awoke of a morning to see the city of Sarras afore them. Here they landed, and took out of the ship the table of silver, Percivale and Bors going tofore and Galahad behind. Right so they went to the city, and at the gate of the city they saw an old bent man. Then Galahad called him, and bade him help to bear this heavy thing.

"Truly," said the old man, "it is ten years since I might go without crutches."

"Care thou not," said Galahad; "arise up and show thy good will."

So he assayed, and found himself as whole as ever he was. Then ran he to the table, and took one part opposite Galahad.

Anon arose there great noise in the city, that a cripple was made whole by knights marvellous that entered into the city. When the king of the city, which was called Estorause, saw the fellowship, he asked them from whence they were, and what thing it was that they had brought upon the table of silver. And they told him the truth of the Holy Grail, and the power which God had set there.

Now King Estorause was a tyrant, and was come of a line of pagans. He took the three knights and put them in a deep hole. But as soon as they were there our Lord sent them the Holy Grail, through whose grace they were always satisfied while that they were in prison.

At the year's end it befell that this king lay sick, and felt that he should die. Then he sent for the three knights. They came afore him, and he cried them mercy of that he had done to them, and they forgave it him goodly, and he died anon.

When the king was dead, all the city was dismayed, and wist not who might be their king. Right so as they were in counsel, there came a voice among them, and bade them choose the youngest knight of them there to be their king, for he should well maintain them and all theirs. So they made Galahad king by all the assent of the whole city.

When he was come to behold the land, he let make about the table of silver a chest of gold and of precious stones that covered the holy vessel; and every day early the three fellows would come afore it and make their prayers.

Now at the year's end the three knights arose early and came to the palace, and saw before them the holy vessel, and a man kneeling, in likeness of a bishop, that had about him a great fellowship of angels. And he called Galahad and said to him, "Come forth, thou servant of Jesu Christ, and thou shalt see that thou hast much desired to see."

Then Galahad began to tremble right hard, when the deadly flesh began to behold the spiritual things. Then he held up his hands towards heaven, and said, "Lord, I thank Thee, for now I see what hath been my desire many a day. Now, blessed Lord, would I not longer live, if it might please thee, Lord."

Therewith the good man took the sacrament and proffered it to Galahad, and he received it right gladly and meekly.

"Now, wotest thou what I am?" said the good man; "I am Joseph of Arimathea, which our Lord hath sent here to thee to bear thee fellowship. And wotest thou wherefore He hath sent me more than any other? For thou hast resembled me in two things, in that thou hast seen the marvels of the Holy Grail, and in that thou hast been a clean and virtuous knight, as I have been and am."

When these words had been spoken, Galahad went to Percivale and to Bors and kissed them and commended them to God, and said, "Salute me to my lord Sir Launcelot, and bid him remember of this unstable world."

Therewith he kneeled down tofore the table and made his prayers, and then suddenly his soul departed to Jesu Christ, and a great multitude of angels bare his soul up to heaven, and the two fellows might well behold it. Also they saw come from heaven a hand, but they saw not the body; and it came right to the vessel, and took it, and bare it up to heaven. Since then was there never man so hard as to say that he had seen the Holy Grail.

When Percivale and Bors saw Galahad had died, they made as much sorrow as ever did two men; and if they had not been good men, they might lightly have fallen in despair. And the people of the country and of the city were right heavy. And then he was buried. And as soon as he was buried, Sir Percivale betook himself to a hermitage out of the city, where for a year and two months he lived a full holy life, and then passed out of this world.

When Bors saw that he was alone in so far countries, he departed from Sarras and came to the sea. There he entered into a ship, and so it befell that in good adventure he came into the realm of Logris. And he rode to Camelot, where King Arthur was, and then was there great joy made of him in the court, for they believed all that he was dead, forasmuch as he had been so long out of the country.

When they had eaten, the King made great clerks to come afore him, that they should chronicle of the high adventures of the good knights. When Bors had told of the adventures of the Holy Grail, such as had befallen him and his two fellows, that was Percivale and Galahad, then

Launcelot told the adventures of the Holy Grail that he had seen. All this was made in great books, and put in chests at Salisbury.

[1] Rivage: bank; shore.

Sir Launcelot and the Fair Maid of Astolat

After the quest of the Holy Grail was fulfilled, and all knights that were left alive were come again unto the Table Round, then was there great joy in the court, and in especial King Arthur and Queen Guenever made great joy of the remnant that were come home. Passing glad were the King and the Queen of Sir Launcelot and of Sir Bors, for they had been long away in the quest of the Holy Grail.

Then, as the book saith, Sir Launcelot began to resort unto Queen Guenever again, and forgat the promise that he made in the quest. For, had he not been in his privy thoughts and in his mind so set inwardly to the Queen, as he was in seeming outward to God, there had no knight passed him in the quest of the Holy Grail. But ever his thoughts were privily on the Queen, more than toforehand, so that many in the court spake of it, and in especial Sir Agravaine, Sir Gawaine's brother, for he was ever open mouthed.

Thus it passed forth till on a day the King let cry great jousts and a tournament that should be at Camelot, that is Winchester, and thither came many knights. So King Arthur made him ready to depart to these jousts, and would have had the Queen with him, but she would not go, pretending to be sick. This grieved the King, for such a fellowship of knights had not been seen together since the Whitsuntide when Galahad departed from the court. And many deemed the Queen would not be there because of Sir Launcelot of the Lake, who would not ride with the King, for he said he was not whole of a wound.

So when the King was departed, the Queen called Sir Launcelot unto her, and told him he was greatly to blame, thus to hold himself behind his lord, and counselled him to take his way towards the tournament at Winchester. So upon the morn he took his leave of the Queen, and departed. He rode all that day, and at eventide he came to Astolat, that is Gilford, and was lodged at the place of an old baron, named Sir Bernard of Astolat. The old knight welcomed him in the best manner, but he knew not that he was Sir Launcelot.

"Fair sir," said Sir Launcelot to his host, "I would pray you to lend me a shield that is not openly known, for mine be well known, and I would go to the tournament in disguise."

"Sir," said his host, "ye shall have your desire, for me seemeth ye be one of the likeliest knights of the world, and I shall show you friendship. Sir, wit ye well I have two sons which were but late made knights. The eldest is called Sir Tirre, and he was hurt that same day that he was made knight, so that he may not ride. His shield ye shall have, for that is not known, I dare say, except in this place. And my youngest son is named Sir Lavaine, and if it please you, he shall ride with you unto the jousts, for he is of his age strong and brave. Much my heart leads me to believe that ye should be a noble knight; therefore I pray you tell me your name."

"As for that," said Sir Launcelot, "ye must hold me excused at his time, but if God give me grace to speed well at the jousts, I shall come again and tell you. But I pray you in any wise let me have your son Sir Lavaine with me, and his brother's shield."

"This shall be done," said Sir Bernard.

This old baron had a daughter, Elaine le Blank, that was called at that time the Fair Maid of Astolat. Ever she beheld Sir Launcelot admiringly, and, as the book saith, she cast such a love unto him that she could never withdraw her love, so she besought him to wear at the jousts a token of hers. "Fair damsel," said Sir Launcelot, "if I grant you that, ye may say I do more for your love than ever I did for lady or damsel."

[Illustration: Elaine]

Then he remembered that he would go to the jousts disguised; and because he had never afore that time borne any manner of token of any damsel, he bethought him that he would bear one of her, so that none of his blood thereby might know him. And then he said, "Fair maiden, I will grant you to wear a token of yours upon my helmet; therefore, show me what it is."

"Sir," she said, "it is a red sleeve of mine, of scarlet, well embroidered with great pearls."

So she brought it him, and Sir Launcelot received it, saying that he had never done so much for any damsel. Then he left his shield in the fair maiden's keeping, and prayed her to care for it until that he came again.

So that night he had merry rest and great cheer, for ever the damsel Elaine was about Sir Launcelot, all the while she might be suffered.

On the morn Sir Launcelot and Sir Lavaine took their leave of Sir Bernard, the old baron, and of his daughter, the Fair Maiden of Astolat, and then they rode so long till they came to Camelot. There was great press of kings, dukes, earls, and barons, and many noble knights; but there Sir Launcelot was lodged privily, by the means of Sir Lavaine, with a rich burgess, so that no man in that town was ware what they were.

At the time appointed the jousts began, and Sir Launcelot made him ready in his best manner, and put the red sleeve upon his head, and fastened it fast. Then he with Sir Lavaine came in at the thickest of the press, and did marvellous deeds of arms, so that all wondered what knight he might be. Sir Gawaine said it might be Sir Launcelot by his riding and his buffets, but ever it seemed it should not be he, for he bore the red sleeve upon his head, and he never wist Sir Launcelot bear token of lady or gentleman at any jousts.

At the last by misfortune Sir Bors unhorsed Sir Launcelot, and smote him through the shield into the side; and the spear brake, and the head was left still in his side. But Sir Lavaine by great force took the horse from the King of Scots and brought it to his lord, Sir Launcelot, and in spite of them all he made him to mount upon that horse. Then Launcelot gat a spear in his hand, and then he smote Sir Bors horse and man to the earth. In the same wise served he other knights, and, as the book saith, he might have slain them, but his heart might not serve him thereto, and he left them there.

Then afterwards he hurled in the thickest press of them all, and did there the marvellousest deeds of arms that ever man saw or heard speak of; and ever Sir Lavaine, the good knight, was with him. And there Sir Launcelot with his sword smote and pulled down, as the French book maketh mention, more than thirty knights, and the most part were of the Table Round. And Sir Lavaine also did full well that day.

At the last the King blew unto lodging, and the prize was given by heralds unto the knight with the white shield, that bare the red sleeve. But Sir Launcelot was sore hurt, and cared not for honour; and groaning piteously, he rode at a great gallop away-ward from all the knights, until he came under a wood's side. When he saw that he was from the field nigh a mile, so that he was sure he might not be seen, he besought Sir Lavaine as he loved him to draw the truncheon out of his side. This Sir Lavaine dreaded sore to do, lest Sir Launcelot should be in peril of death from loss of blood, if the truncheon were drawn out. Yet he did as his lord would have him do, and Sir Launcelot gave a great shriek, and so swooned pale and deadly.

Thereupon Sir Lavaine took him to a hermitage fast by within two miles, where dwelt a gentle hermit, that sometime was a full noble knight and a great lord of possessions. For great goodness he had taken himself to wilful poverty, and forsaken many lands. He was a full noble surgeon, and anon he stanched Sir Launcelot's blood, and made him to drink good wine, so that he was well refreshed, and came to himself.

Meanwhile King Arthur let seek the knight that bare the red sleeve, that he might have his laud and honour, and the prize, as was right. But he could not be found, and the King and all the knights feared he was sore hurt in the battle. Then Sir Gawaine took a squire with him and drove all about Camelot within six or seven miles, but could hear no word of him.

Then within two days King Arthur and all the fellowship returned unto London again, and so, as they rode by the way, it happened that Sir Gawaine was lodged at Astolat with Sir Bernard. There by the means of the shield left in Elaine's care he learned that the knight who won such honour at the tournament was none other than Sir Launcelot himself, and the Fair Maid of Astolat learned on how valiant a knight she had fixed her love.

When Elaine heard also that Sir Launcelot was grievously wounded and that the knights knew not where he lay, she said to Sir Bernard, her father: "Now I request you give me leave to ride and to seek him, or else I wot well I shall go out of my mind, for I shall never stop till that I find him and my brother, Sir Lavaine."

"Do as it liketh you," said her father, "for I am right sore grieved of the hurt of that noble knight."

Right so the maid made herself ready, and Sir Gawaine rode on to London, where he openly disclosed to all the court that it was Sir Launcelot that bore the red sleeve, and that jousted best. And when Sir Bors heard that, wit ye well he was a heavy man, and so were all his kinsmen, for it was he who had given Sir Launcelot, that was his own cousin, the grievous wound in the tournament. But when Queen Guenever wist that Sir Launcelot bare the red sleeve of the Fair Maid of Astolat, she was nigh out of her mind for wrath, and called him false traitor, because he had worn the token of any lady but herself.

As fair Elaine came to Winchester, she sought there all about, and by fortune Sir Lavaine had ridden out to refresh himself and to exercise his horse. Anon as Elaine saw him she knew him, and then she cried aloud unto him. When he heard her, anon he came hither, and then she asked her brother how Sir Launcelot did.

"Who told you, sister," said he, "that my lord's name is Sir Launcelot?"

Then she told him how Sir Gawaine knew him by his shield, and so they rode together till they came to the hermitage. Anon she alighted, and Sir Lavaine brought her in to Sir Launcelot. So this maiden, Elaine, never went from Sir Launcelot, but watched him day and night, and did such attendance to him that the French book saith there was never woman did kindlier for man than she.

After a long while he was healed of his wounds, and so upon a morn they took their horses, and Elaine le Blank with them, and departed from the hermit. And when they came to Astolat, there they were well lodged, and had great cheer of Sir Bernard the old baron, and of Sir Tirre his son.

When Sir Launcelot should depart from Astolat for to return to King Arthur's court, fair Elaine seemed like to die for love of him and for sorrow at his going. But Sir Launcelot loved only Queen Guenever, and thought never to be wedded man, and could only grieve at her great sorrow; and for her good will and great kindness he promised that, whensoever she should set her heart upon some good knight that would wed her, he would give her a thousand pounds yearly, and always while he lived be her own true knight.

Then Sir Launcelot took his leave, and with Sir Lavaine he came unto Winchester. And when Arthur wist that Sir Launcelot was come whole and sound, he made great joy of him, and so did all the knights of the Round Table except Sir Agravaine and Sir Mordred.

Now speak we of the Fair Maiden of Astolat, that made such sorrow day and night that she never slept, ate, or drank, and ever she made her lament for Sir Launcelot. When she had thus endured a ten days, and weakened so that she must needs pass out of this world, she prepared for death, but ever she mourned for Sir Launcelot.

Then her priest bade her leave such thoughts; but she said, "Why should I leave such thoughts? Am I not an earthly woman? And all the while the breath is in my body I may lament, for I do none offence, though I love an earthly man, and I take God to my record I never loved any but Sir Launcelot of the Lake, and as I am a pure maiden I never shall. And since it is the sufferance of God that I shall die for the love of so noble a knight, I beseech the High Father of Heaven to have mercy upon my soul; and sweet Lord Jesu, I take Thee to record, I was never great offender against Thy laws, but that I loved this noble knight Sir Launcelot out of measure, and of myself, good Lord, I might not withstand the fervent love wherefore I have my death."

Then she called her father Sir Bernard and her brother Sir Tirre, and heartily she prayed her father that her brother might write a letter like as she did endite it, and so her father granted her. And when the letter was written word by word as she devised, then she prayed her father that after her death she might be put in a barge in all her richest clothes, the letter fast in her right hand, and that the barge, covered over and over with black samite, might be steered by one boatman only down the Thames to Westminster.

So she died, and all was done as she desired. Now by fortune King Arthur and Queen Guenever were speaking together at a window of the palace, and as they looked they espied this black barge, and had marvel what it meant. And the King sent three knights thither to bring him ready word what was there. Then these three knights came to the barge, and found therein the fairest corpse lying in a rich bed, and a poor man sitting at the barge's end, and no word would he speak. Then the King took the Queen by the hand and went thither, and there they saw the fair woman in all the rich clothing lying as though she smiled. And the Queen espied the letter in her right hand, and a clerk read it in the presence of many knights.

This was the intent of the letter: "Most noble knight Sir Launcelot, now hath death made us two at debate for your love. I was your lover, that men called the Fair Maiden of Astolat; therefore unto all ladies I make my moan; yet pray for my soul, and bury me at the least, and offer my mass-penny. This is my last request. And a clean maiden I died, I take God to witness. Pray for my soul, Sir Launcelot, as thou art peerless."

When the letter was read, the King, the Queen, and all the knights wept for pity at the doleful lament. Then was Sir Launcelot sent for, and when he heard the letter word by word, he said: "My lord Arthur, wit ye well I am right heavy of the death of this fair damsel, but God knoweth I was never cause of her death by my willing. I will not say but that she was both fair and good, and much I was beholden unto her, but she loved me out of measure."

Then said the King unto Sir Launcelot, "It will be your honour that ye oversee that she be interred honourably."

"Sir," said Sir Launcelot, "that shall be done as I can best devise."

So upon the morn she was interred richly, and Sir Launcelot offered her mass-penny, and all the knights of the Table Round that were there at that time offered with Sir Launcelot.

And the Queen sent for Sir Launcelot, and prayed him of mercy, because she had been wroth with him causeless, and he willingly forgave her.

So it passed on all that winter with all manner of hunting and hawking, and jousts and tourneys were many betwixt the great lords; and ever in all places Sir Lavaine gat great honour, so that he was nobly renowned among many knights of the Table Round.

Of the Great Tournament on Candlemas Day

At Christmas time many knights were together at the court, and every day there was a joust made. Sir Lavaine jousted there all that Christmas passing well, and was praised best, for there were but few that did so well. Wherefore all knights thought that Sir Lavaine should be made knight of the Round Table at the next feast of Pentecost.

But Sir Launcelot would joust only when a great tournament was held. So after Christmas King Arthur had many knights called unto him, and there they agreed together to make a party and a great tournament near Westminster on Candlemas Day. Of this many knights were glad, and made themselves ready to be at these jousts in the freshest manner. The Queen Guenever sent for Sir Launcelot, and said: "At these jousts that shall be ye shall bear upon your helmet the sleeve of gold that ye shall have of me, and I pray you, for my sake exert yourself there so that men may speak of your honour."

"Madam," said Sir Launcelot, "it shall be done."

And when Sir Launcelot saw his time, he told Sir Bors that he would depart, and have no others with him than Sir Lavaine, unto the good hermit that dwelt in the forest of Windsor,—his name was Sir Brastias,—and there he intended to take all the repose he might, because he wished to be fresh on the day of the jousts.

So Sir Launcelot with Sir Lavaine departed so quietly that no creature except the noble men of his own kin knew what had become of him. And when he had come to the hermitage, you may be sure he had good cheer. Daily he would go to a spring hard by the hermitage, and there he would lie down and watch the spring bubble, and sometimes he slept there.

At that time a lady dwelt in the forest, who was a great huntress. Every day she used to hunt, and no men ever went with her, but always women. They were all shooters, and could well kill a deer both under cover and in the open. They always carried bows and arrows, horns and wood-knives, and many good dogs they had.

Now it happened that this lady, the huntress, was one day chasing a deer, keeping the direction by the noise of the hounds. The deer, hard pressed, came down to the spring where Sir Launcelot was sleeping, and there sank down exhausted, and lay there a great while. At length the dogs came fast after, and beat about, for they had lost the very perfect track of the deer. Just then there came that lady, the huntress, who knew by the sounds of the dogs that the deer must be at the spring. So she came swiftly and found the deer. She put a broad arrow in her bow, and shot at it, but aimed too high, and so by misfortune the arrow smote Sir Launcelot deep in the thick of the thigh. When Sir Launcelot felt himself so hurt, he jumped up madly, and saw the lady that had smitten him. And when he saw it was a woman, he said thus; "Lady or damsel, whatever thou be, in an evil time ye bare a bow; the devil made you a shooter."

"Now mercy, fair sir," said the lady; "I am a gentlewoman that am wont to hunt here in this forest, and truly I saw you not; there was the deer by the spring, and I believed I was doing well to shoot, but my hand swerved."

"Alas," said Sir Launcelot, "ye have done mischief to me."

And so the lady departed, and Sir Launcelot, as well as he might, pulled out the arrow, but the head remained still in his thigh; and so he went feebly to the hermitage, ever bleeding as he went. And when Sir Lavaine and the hermit spied that Sir Launcelot was hurt, wit ye well they were passing sorry; but neither Sir Lavaine nor the hermit knew how he was hurt, or by whom. Then with great pain the hermit gat the arrow's head out of Sir Launcelot's thigh, but much of his blood was shed, and the wound was passing sore.

"Ah, mercy," said Sir Launcelot, "I call myself the most unhappy man that liveth; for ever when I would most gladly have honour there befalleth me some unhappy thing. Now, so heaven help me, I shall be in the field upon Candlemas Day at the jousts, whatsoever come of it."

So all that might heal Sir Launcelot was gotten, and, when the day came, he and Sir Lavaine had themselves and their horses arrayed, and so departed and came nigh to the field. Many proved good knights with their retainers were there ready to joust, and King Arthur himself came into the field with two hundred knights, the most part noble knights of the Table Round. And there were old knights set in scaffolds, for to judge with the Queen who did best.

Then they blew to the field, and the knights met in the battle, furiously smiting down one and another in the rush of the tournament. King Arthur himself ran into the lists with a hundred followers, smiting to the earth four knights, one after the other, and even when his spear was broken he did passing well. And so knight after knight came in,—Sir Gawaine, and Sir Gaheris, and Sir Agravaine, and Sir Mordred, and many others; all pressed their opponents hard, some being discomfited and others gaining great honour by their mighty prowess.

All this doing Sir Launcelot saw, and then he came into the field with Sir Lavaine, as if it had been thunder. He encountered with Sir Gawaine, and by force smote him and his horse to the earth, and then one knight after another all with one spear. And Sir Lavaine encountered with Sir Palamides, and either met other so hard and so fiercely that both their horses fell to the earth. But they were horsed again, and then Sir Launcelot met with Sir Palamides, and there Sir Palamides had a fall. And so Sir Launcelot, as fast as he could get spears, smote down thirty knights, and the most part of them were knights of the Table Round. And then King Arthur was wroth when he saw Sir Launcelot do such deeds, and with nine chosen knights made ready to set upon Sir Launcelot and Sir Lavaine.

All this espied Sir Gareth, and he said to Sir Bors, "I will ride unto my lord Sir Launcelot for to help him, fall of it what may, for he is the same man that made me knight."

"Ye shall not so," said Sir Bors, "by my counsel, unless ye be disguised."

"Ye shall see me disguised," said Sir Gareth.

So he rode to a Welsh knight who lay to repose himself, for he was sore hurt afore by Sir Gawaine, and Sir Gareth prayed him of his knighthood to lend him his green shield for his.

"I will well," said the Welsh knight.

So Sir Gareth came driving to Sir Launcelot with all his might, and bore him fellowship for old love he had shown him. And so the King and his nine knights encountered with Sir Launcelot and Sir Lavaine and Sir Gareth. And Sir Gareth did such deeds of arms that all men wondered what knight he was with the green shield; for he smote down that day and pulled down more than thirty knights. Also Sir Launcelot knew not Sir Gareth, and marvelled, when he beheld him do such deeds, what knight he might be.

So this tournament and this joust lasted long, till it was near evening, for the knights of the Round Table ever came to the relief of King Arthur, who was wroth out of measure that he and his knights could not prevail that day over Sir Launcelot and the knights who were with him.

So when they had long dealt one another great strokes and neither might prevail, King Arthur said to Sir Gawaine, "Tell me now, nephew, what is your best counsel?"

"Sir," said Sir Gawaine, "ye shall have my counsel. Have sounded the call unto lodging, for, trust me, truly it will be of no avail to strive with Sir Launcelot of the Lake and my brother, Sir Gareth,—for he it is with the green shield,—helped as they are by that good young knight, Sir Lavaine, unless we should fall ten or twelve upon one knight, and that would be no honour, but shame."

"Ye say truth," said the King, "and it were shame to us, so many as we are, to set upon them any more."

So then they blew unto lodging, and King Arthur rode after Sir Launcelot and prayed him and other of the knights to supper.

So they went unto Arthur's lodging all together, and there was a great feast and great revel, and the prize was given unto Sir Launcelot. Then Sir Launcelot told the King and the Queen how the lady huntress shot him in the forest of Windsor in the thigh with a broad arrow. Also Arthur blamed Sir Gareth, because he left his fellowship and held with Sir Launcelot.

"My lord," said Sir Gareth, "he made me a knight, and when I saw him so hard bestead, me thought it was my honour to help him, for I saw him do so much, and I was ashamed to see so many noble knights against him alone."

"Truly," said King Arthur unto Sir Gareth, "ye say well, and honourably have ye done, and all the days of my life be sure I shall love you and trust you the more for the great honour ye have done to yourself. For ever it is an honourable knight's duty to help another honourable knight when he seeth him in a great danger, for ever an honourable man will be loath to see an honourable man put to shame. He that is of no honour, and fareth with cowardice, will never show gentleness nor any manner of goodness where he seeth a man in any danger, for never will a coward show any mercy, and always a good man will do to another man as he would be done to himself."

So then there were great feasts unto kings and dukes; and revel, game, and play, and all manner of nobleness was used; and he that was courteous, true, and faithful to his friend was at that time cherished.

Queen Guenever's May-Day Ride and What Came of it

Thus it passed on from Candlemas until after Easter, and soon the month of May was come, when every manly heart begins to blossom and to bring forth fruit. For as herbs and trees flourish in May, likewise every lusty heart springeth and flourisheth in lusty deeds, for more than any other month May giveth unto all men renewed courage, and calleth again to their mind old gentleness and old service, and many kind deeds that were forgotten by negligence. Therefore, as the month of May flowereth and flourisheth in many gardens, so let every man of honour bring forth fruit in his heart, first unto God, and next unto the joy of them to whom he has promised his faith.

So it befell in the month of May that Queen Guenever called unto her ten knights of the Table Round, and she bade them ride with her a-Maying on the morrow into the woods and fields near Westminster. And "I bid you," said she, "that ye all be well horsed, and that ye all be clothed in green, either silk or woollen, and I shall bring with me ten ladies, and every knight shall have a lady behind him, and every knight shall have a squire and two yeomen."

So they made themselves ready in the freshest manner, and in the morning rode with the Queen a-Maying in woods and meadows as it pleased them in great joy and delight. The Queen purposed to be again with King Arthur at the furthest by ten of the clock.

Now there was a knight called Meliagrance, who had at that time a castle, the gift of King Arthur, within seven miles of Westminster. He had long lain in wait to steal away the Queen, but had feared to do the base deed when Sir Launcelot was in her company. It was her custom at that time never to ride without a great fellowship of men of arms about her, for the most part young men eager for honour, and called the Queen's knights. But this knight, Sir Meliagrance, had espied the Queen well and her purpose on this May morning, and had seen how Sir Launcelot was not with her, and how she had for this once no men of arms with her but the ten noble knights all arrayed in green for Maying. Then he provided him twenty men of arms and a hundred archers, to destroy the Queen's knights, for he thought that time was the best season to take the Queen prisoner.

So while the Queen and all her knights were gathering herbs and mosses and flowers in the best manner and freshest, just then there came out of a wood Sir Meliagrance with eight-score men, well armed, and bade the Queen and her knights to stand.

"Traitor knight," said Queen Guenever, "what intendest thou to do? Wilt thou shame thyself? Bethink thee how thou art a king's son, and knight of the Table Round, and thou art about to dishonour the noble king that made thee knight; thou shamest all knighthood and thyself; but me, I let thee wit, thou shalt never shame, for I had rather cut my throat in twain than that thou shouldst dishonour me."

"As for all this language," said Sir Meliagrance, "be it as it may, never before could I get you at such advantage as I do now, and therefore I will take you as I find you."

All the ten noble knights sought to dissuade him from dishonouring himself and from forcing them to jeopard their lives, unarmed as they were, in defending the Queen. But Sir Meliagrance would not yield, and the ten knights of the Table Round drew their swords and stood manly against the spears and swords of the others. But Sir Meliagrance had them at great advantage, and anon six of them were smitten to the earth with grimly wounds. The other four fought long, but at last they also were sore wounded.

When the Queen saw that her knights needs must be slain at the last, she for pity and sorrow agreed to go with Sir Meliagrance to his castle upon this covenant, that he suffer not her knights to be more hurt, and that they be led wheresoever she was taken. "For," said she, "I will rather slay myself than go with thee, unless these my noble knights may be in my presence."

Meliagrance consented, and by the Queen's commandment they left battle. The wounded knights were placed on horseback, some sitting, some across the horses' backs in a pitiful manner, and all rode in haste to the castle. Then Sir Meliagrance charged the Queen and all her knights that no one should depart from her, for full sore he dreaded Sir Launcelot, lest he should have any knowledging.

But the Queen privily called unto her a page who could ride swiftly, gave him her ring, and told him to bear it, when he saw a chance to slip away quietly, unto Sir Launcelot of the Lake, and pray him to rescue her. "And spare thou not thy horse," said she, "neither for water nor for land."

So the page espied his time, and lightly he touched his horse with the spurs, and departed as fast as he might. Sir Meliagrance saw him so flee, and understood that it was to warn Sir Launcelot. Then they that were best horsed chased him and shot at him, but he escaped them all, and anon found Sir Launcelot. And when he had told his message, and delivered him the Queen's ring, "Alas," said Sir Launcelot, "now am I shamed forever, unless that I may rescue that noble lady from dishonour."

Then he eagerly called for his armour, and ever the page told him how the ten knights had fought marvellously, till at last the Queen made appointment to go with Sir Meliagrance for to save their lives.

"Alas," said Sir Launcelot, "that most noble lady, that she should be so destroyed! I would give all France to have been there well armed."

So when Sir Launcelot was armed and upon his horse, he sent the Queen's page to tell Sir Lavaine how suddenly he had departed, and for what cause, and to pray him to come anon to the castle where Sir Meliagrance abideth.

Sir Launcelot, it is said, took to the water at Westminster bridge and made his horse swim over the Thames to Lambeth; and then he rode as fast as he might, until within a while he came to the place where the ten knights had fought with Sir Meliagrance. He then followed the path until he came to a straight way through the wood. Here he was stopped by thirty archers that Sir Meliagrance had sent out to slay Sir Launcelot's horse, but in no wise to have ado with him bodily, "for," he had said, "he is overhard to overcome." These archers bade Sir Launcelot to turn again and follow no longer that track, and when Sir Launcelot gave right naught for them, then they shot his horse, and smote him with many arrows. Sir Launcelot now set out on foot, but there were so many ditches and hedges betwixt the archers and him that he could not meddle with any one of them.

He went on a while, but was much cumbered by his armour, his shield, and his spear. Wit ye well he was sore annoyed at his slow progress, but was loath to leave anything that belonged unto him, for he dreaded sore the treason of Sir Meliagrance.

Just then by chance there came by a cart, that was sent thither to fetch wood. "Tell me, carter," said Sir Launcelot, "what shall I give thee to take me in thy cart unto a castle within two miles of here?"

"Thou shalt not set foot in my cart," said the man, "for I am sent to fetch wood for my lord Sir Meliagrance."

Then Sir Launcelot jumped upon him and gave the man such a blow that he fell to the earth stark dead. Then the other carter, his fellow, was afraid of going the same way, and cried out, "Fair lord, save my life and I will bring you where ye will."

Sir Launcelot leaped into the cart, and the carter drove at a great gallop, Sir Launcelot's horse following after with more than forty arrows in him.

More than an hour and a half later, Queen Guenever was in a bay window of the castle with her ladies, and espied an armed knight approaching, standing in a cart.

"See, madam," said a lady to her, "there rideth in a cart a goodly armed knight; I suppose he rideth to hanging."

Then the Queen espied by his shield that Sir Launcelot of the Lake himself was there. "Alas," said the Queen; "now I see that well is it with him who hath a trusty friend. Ah, most noble knight, I see well thou are hard bestead, when thou ridest in a cart."

By this time Sir Launcelot had come to the gates of that castle, and there he descended from the cart, and cried so that all the castle rang: "Where art thou, false traitor Sir Meliagrance, and knight of the Table Round? Now come forth here, thou traitor knight, thou and thy fellowship with thee, for here I am, Sir Launcelot of the Lake, that shall fight with thee."

With these words he burst the gate wide open upon the porter, and smote him under his ear with his gauntlet so that he staggered back like a dead man. When Sir Meliagrance heard that Sir Launcelot was there, he ran unto Queen Guenever and fell upon his knees, putting himself wholly at her mercy, and begging her to control the wrath of Sir Launcelot.

"Better is peace than ever war," said the Queen, "and the less noise the more is my honour."

So she and her ladies went down to Sir Launcelot, thanked him for all his trouble in her behalf, told him of Meliagrance's repentance, and bade him come in peaceably with her.

"Madam," said Sir Launcelot, "if ye are accorded with him, I am not inclined to be against peace, howbeit Sir Meliagrance hath done full shamefully to me, and cowardly. Ah, madam, had I known ye would be so soon accorded with him, I would not have made such haste unto you."

"What," said the Queen, "do ye repent of your good deeds? Wit ye well I never made peace with him for labour or love that I had unto him, but to suppress all shameful noise."

"Madam," said Sir Launcelot, "ye understand full well I was never glad of shameful slander nor noise; and there is neither king, queen, nor knight alive except my lord King Arthur and you, madam, that should hinder me from making Sir Meliagrance's heart full cold or ever I departed from hence."

Then the Queen and Sir Launcelot went in together, and she commanded him to be unarmed. Then he asked where the ten knights were that were wounded sore. So she led Sir Launcelot to them, and they made great joy of his coming, and he made great dole of their hurts, and bewailed them greatly. And then Sir Launcelot told them how he had been obliged to put himself into a cart. Thus they complained each to other, and full gladly would they have been revenged, but they restrained themselves because of the Queen. So Sir Launcelot was called for many a day thereafter the Chevalier of the Cart, and he did many deeds, and great adventures he had. And so we leave this tale of the Knight of the Cart, and turn to others.

Of the Plot Against Sir Launcelot

In this same month of May when every lusty heart flourisheth and bourgeoneth, there befell in King Arthur's realm a great anger and ill fortune that stinted not till the flower of chivalry of all the world was destroyed. And all was due to two evil knights, the which were named Sir Agravaine and Sir Mordred, that were nephews unto King Arthur and brethren unto Sir Gawaine. For this Sir Agravaine and Sir Mordred had ever a privy hate unto the Queen, Dame Guenever, and to Sir Launcelot, and daily and nightly they ever watched upon him.

So it mishapped that Sir Agravaine on a day said openly, so that many knights might hear, that the friendship between Sir Launcelot and the Queen was a disgrace to knighthood and a shame to so noble a king as Arthur. But Sir Gawaine would not hear any of these tales nor be of Agravaine's counsel; moreover he charged his brother to move no such matters afore him, for he wist well what mischief would come, should war arise betwixt Sir Launcelot and the King, and he remembered how ofttimes Sir Launcelot had proved his goodness and loyalty by knightly deeds. Also Sir Gaheris and Sir Gareth, two other brethren, would know nothing of Agravaine's base accusation.

But Sir Mordred, the fifth of the brethren, sons of the Queen of Orkney, the which had mocked the good Percivale when first he came to the court, and who had ever been jealous and ready to think evil of another, joined with Sir Agravaine. Therewithal they three, Sir Gawaine, Sir Gaheris, and Sir Gareth departed, making great dole over the mischief that threatened the destruction of the realm and the dispersion of the noble fellowship of the Round Table.

So Sir Agravaine and Sir Mordred came before King Arthur, and told him they might no longer suffer Sir Launcelot's deeds, for he was a traitor to his kingly person. But the King would believe nothing unless he might have proofs of it, for, as the French book saith, he was full loath to hear ill of a knight who had done so much for him and for the Queen so many times that, as was fully known, he loved him passingly well.

Then these two brethren made a plot for taking Sir Launcelot when in the Queen's presence, and bringing him dead or quick to King Arthur. So on the morn Sir Agravaine and Sir Mordred gat to them twelve knights and hid themselves in a chamber in the castle of Carlisle, where Queen Guenever was; thus they plotted to take Sir Launcelot by force, if she should have speech with him. Sir Launcelot was no coward, and cared not what liars said about him, since he wist his own good will and loyalty. So when the Queen sent for him to speak with her, he went as true knight to the castle, and fell into the trap that was set for him. In the battle that followed he was hard bestead, but slew Sir Agravaine at the first buffet, and within a little while he laid the twelve chosen knights cold to the earth. Also he wounded Sir Mordred, who, when he escaped from the noble Sir Launcelot, anon gat his horse and rode unto King Arthur, sore wounded and all bleeding.

Then he told the King how it was, and how they were all slain save himself only. So the King believed Sir Mordred's evil accusation true, and he said: "Alas, me sore repenteth that ever Sir Launcelot should be against me. Now am I sure the noble fellowship of the Round Table is broken for ever, for with him will many a noble knight hold. And now it is fallen so that I may not keep my honour unless the Queen suffer the death."

So then there was made great ordinance that the Queen must be judged to the death, for the law was such in those days that whatsoever they were, of what estate or degree, if they were found guilty of treason, there should be none other remedy but death. Right so it was ordained for Queen Guenever, and she was commanded to the fire, there to be burned.

King Arthur prayed Sir Gawaine to make himself ready in his best armour, with his brethren Sir Gaheris and Sir Gareth, to bring the Queen to the fire, there to have her judgment, and receive the death. But Sir Gawaine ever believed Dame Guenever guiltless of the treason charged against her, and he would never have it said that he had any part in her shameful end. Sir Gaheris and Sir Gareth also were loath to be there present, but they were young, and full unable to say him nay. "If we be there by your straight commandment," said they, "ye shall plainly hold us excused though we go in peaceable wise, and bear none harness of war upon us."

So the Queen was led forth without Carlisle, and she prepared herself for death. There was weeping and wailing and wringing of hands of many lords and ladies, and few in comparison there present would bear any armour for to keep order.

Anon as the fire was to be lighted, there was spurring and plucking up of horses, and right so Sir Launcelot and his followers came hither, and whoever stood against them was slain. And so in this rushing and hurling, as Sir Launcelot pressed here and there, it mishapped him to slay Gaheris and Gareth, the noble knights, for they were unarmed and unaware. In truth Sir Launcelot saw them not, and so were they found dead among the thickest of the press.

Then when Sir Launcelot had thus done, and had slain or put to flight all that would withstand him, he rode straight unto Dame Guenever, and made her to be set behind him on his horse, and prayed her to be of good cheer. Wit ye well the Queen was glad that she was escaped from the death, and then she thanked God and Sir Launcelot.

And so he rode his way with the Queen, as the French book saith, unto Joyous Gard, his own castle, where Sir Tristram had taken the Fair Isoud after her flight from Cornwall. There Sir Launcelot kept Guenever as a noble knight should do, and many great lords and some kings sent him many good knights, and many noble knights drew unto Sir Launcelot.

When it was known openly that King Arthur and Sir Launcelot were at debate, many were full heavy of heart, and the King himself swooned for pure sorrow, as it was told him how and in what wise the Queen was taken away from the fire, and as he heard of the death of his noble knights, in especial that of Sir Gaheris and Sir Gareth. And when he awoke of his swoon, he said: "Alas that ever I bare crown upon my head, for now have I lost the fairest fellowship of noble knights that ever Christian king held together. Alas that ever this war began. The death of these two brethren will cause the greatest mortal war that ever was, for I am sure, wist Sir Gawaine that Sir Gareth were slain, I should never have rest of him till I had destroyed Sir Launcelot's kin and himself, or else he had destroyed me. Ah, Agravaine, Agravaine, Jesu forgive it thy soul, for the evil will thou and thy brother Sir Mordred haddest unto Sir Launcelot hath caused all this sorrow."

How Sir Launcelot Departed from the King and from Joyous Gard

There came one unto Sir Gawaine, and told him how the Queen was led away by Sir Launcelot, and nigh a twenty-four knights slain.

"Full well wist I," said then Sir Gawaine, "that Sir Launcelot would rescue her, or else he would die in that field. To say the truth, had he not rescued the Queen he would not have been a man of honour, inasmuch as she was to have been burned for his sake. He hath done but knightly, and as I would have done myself, had I stood in like case. But where are my brethren? I marvel I hear not of them."

Then the man told him that Sir Gareth and Sir Gaheris were slain, both by the hand of Launcelot. "That may I not believe," said Sir Gawaine, "that he slew my brother Sir Gareth, for I dare say Gareth loved him better than me and all his brethren, and the King also. Sir Launcelot made him knight, and had he desired my brother Sir Gareth with him, he would have been with him against the King and us all. Therefore I may never believe that Sir Launcelot slew my brother."

When at the last he knew in truth that Sir Gareth and Sir Gaheris had died by Sir Launcelot's hand, all his joy was gone. He fell down in a swoon, and long he lay there as he had been dead. When he arose of his swoon he ran to the King crying, and weeping, and said: "O King Arthur, my lord and mine uncle, wit ye well, from this day I shall never fail Sir Launcelot, until the one of us have slain the other. Therefore dress you to the war, for wit ye well I will be revenged upon him."

Unto King Arthur now drew many knights, dukes, and earls, so that he had a great host. Then they made them ready to lay siege about Sir Launcelot, where he lay within Joyous Gard. Thereof heard Sir Launcelot, and he gathered together his followers, for with him held many good knights, some for his own sake, and some for the Queen's sake. Thus they were on both sides well furnished and provided with all manner of things that belonged to the war.

But Sir Launcelot was full loath to do battle against the King, and so he withdrew into his strong castle with all manner of victual and as many noble men as might suffice, and for a long time would in no wise ride out, neither would he allow any of his good knights to issue out, though King Arthur with Sir Gawaine came and laid a siege all about Joyous Gard, both at the town and at the castle.

Then it befell upon a day in harvest time, Sir Launcelot looked over the walls, and spake on high unto King Arthur and Sir Gawaine: "My lords both, wit ye well all is in vain that ye make at this siege; here win ye no honour, for if I list to come out with my good knights, I should full soon make an end of this war. But God defend me, that ever I should encounter with the most noble King that made me knight."

"Fie upon thy fair language," said the King; "come forth, if thou darest. Wit thou well, I am thy mortal foe, and ever shall be to my death day, for thou hast slain my good knights and full noble men of my blood, and like a traitor hast taken my Queen from me by force."

"My most noble lord and king," answered Sir Launcelot, "ye may say what ye will, for ye wot well with yourself I will not strive. I wot well that I have slain your good knights, and that me sore repenteth; but I was forced to do battle with them in saving of my life, or else I must have suffered them to slay me. And as for my lady, Queen Guenever, except your highness and my lord Sir Gawaine, there is no knight under heaven that dare make it good upon me, that ever I was traitor unto your person, and I will prove it upon any knight alive, except you and Sir Gawaine, that my lady Queen Guenever is as true and loyal unto you as any living unto her lord. Howbeit, it hath pleased her good grace to have me in charity, and to cherish me more than any other knight, and unto my power I in return have deserved her love; for ofttimes, my lord, it fortuned me to do battle for her, and ye thanked me when I saved her life. Now me thinketh ye reward me full ill for my good service, and me seemeth I had lost a great part of my honour in my knighthood, had I suffered my lady your queen to be burned, inasmuch as she was to be burned for my sake. For, since I have done battle for your queen in other quarrels than in mine own, me seemeth now I had more right to do battle for her in right quarrel. Therefore, my good and gracious lord, take your queen unto your good grace, for she is both fair, true, and good."

"Fie on thy proud words," said Sir Gawaine; "as for my lady the Queen, I will never say of her shame, but thou false and recreant knight, what cause hadst thou to slay my good brother Sir Gareth, that loved thee more than all my kin? Alas, thou madest him knight with thine own hands; why slewest thou him that loved thee so well?"

"For to excuse myself," said Sir Launcelot, "it helpeth me not, but by the faith I owe to the high order of knighthood, I should with as good will have slain my nephew Sir Bors of Ganis. Alas, that ever I was so unhappy that I had not seen Sir Gareth and Sir Gaheris."

But Sir Gawaine was mischievously set, and it helped not Sir Launcelot to seek accordment. King Arthur must needs unto battle because of his nephew's great anger, and on the morn he was ready in the field with three great hosts. Then Sir Launcelot's fellowship came out at three gates in a full good array, in order and rule as noble knights. And always Sir Launcelot charged all his knights in any wise to save King Arthur and Sir Gawaine.

Then began a great battle, and much people was slain. Ever Sir Launcelot did what he might to save the people on King Arthur's side, and ever King Arthur was nigh about Sir Launcelot to slay him. Sir Launcelot suffered him, and would not strike again; but at the last Sir Bors encountered with King Arthur, and with a spear smote him down. He alighted and drew his sword to slay him, and then he said to Sir Launcelot, "Shall I make an end of this war?"

"Not so hardy," said Sir Launcelot, "upon pain of thy head, touch him no further, for I will never see that most noble king, that made me knight, either slain or shamed."

Therewithal Sir Launcelot alighted oft his horse and took up the King, and horsed him again, and said thus: "My lord Arthur, for God's love stint this strife, for ye get here no honour, if I will to do mine uttermost; always I forbear you, but neither you nor any of yours forbeareth me. My lord, remember what I have done in many places, and now I am evil rewarded."

When King Arthur was again on horseback, he looked upon Sir Launcelot, and then the tears burst out of his eyes, thinking on the great courtesy that was in Sir Launcelot, more than in any other man. Therewith the King might no longer behold him, and he rode his way, saying, "Alas that ever this war began."

And then both sides withdrew to repose themselves, to bury the dead, and to lay soft salves on the wounded. Thus they passed the night, but on the morn they made ready again to do battle. At the end of this day also Sir Launcelot and his party stood better, but for pity he withheld his knights, and suffered King Arthur's party to withdraw one side, and Sir Launcelot again returned into his castle.

So the war went on day after day. It was noised through all Christendom, and at the last it was noised afore the Pope. He, considering the great goodness of King Arthur and of Sir Launcelot, that were called the noblest knights of the world, called unto him a noble clerk, that at that time was there present,—the French book saith it was the Bishop of Rochester,—and gave him bulls unto King Arthur of England, charging him upon pain of interdicting of all England, that he take his queen, Dame Guenever, unto him again, and accord with Sir Launcelot.

So when this bishop was come to Carlisle he showed the King the bulls, and by their means peace was made between King Arthur and Sir Launcelot. With great pomp and ceremony Sir Launcelot rode with the Queen from Joyous Gard to Carlisle, and they knelt before King Arthur, that was full gladly accorded with them both. But Sir Gawaine would never be at peace with the knight that had slain his brethren.

"The King may take his Queen again, if he will," said Sir Gawaine to Sir Launcelot, "and may be accorded with thee, but thou and I are past pardon. Thou shalt go from Carlisle safe, as thou camest, but in this land thou shalt not abide past fifteen days, such summons I give thee;—so the King and I were consented and accorded ere thou camest hither, and else, wit thou well, thou shouldest not have come here except without thy head. If it were not for the Pope's commandment, I should do battle with mine own body against thy body, and prove it upon thee that thou hast been both false unto mine uncle and to me, and that shall I prove upon thy body when thou art departed from hence, wheresoever I find thee."

Then Sir Launcelot sighed, and therewith the tears fell on his cheeks, and he said: "Alas, most noble Christian realm, that I have loved above all others, in thee have I gotten a great part of my honour, and now I shall depart in this wise. Truly me repenteth that ever I came in this realm that I should be thus shamefully banished, undeserved, and causeless. But fortune is so variant, and the wheel so movable, there is no constant abiding. Wit ye well, Sir Gawaine, I may live upon my lands as well as any knight that here is. And if ye, most redoubted King, will come upon my lands with Sir Gawaine, to war upon me, I must endure you as well as I may. But as to you, Sir Gawaine, if that ye come there, I pray you charge me not with treason or felony, for if ye do, I must answer you."

Then Sir Launcelot said unto Guenever, in hearing of the King and them all, "Madam, now I must depart from you and this noble fellowship for ever; and since it is so, I beseech you to pray for me, and say me well; and if ye be hard bestead by any false tongues lightly, my lady, let send me word, and if any knight's hands may deliver you by battle, I shall deliver you."

Therewithal Sir Launcelot kissed the Queen, and then he said all openly: "Now let see what he be in this place, that dare say the Queen is not true unto my lord Arthur; let see who will speak, if he dare."

Then he brought her to the King, and so took his leave and departed. And there was neither king, duke nor earl, baron nor knight, lady nor gentlewoman, but all they wept as people out of their mind, except Sir Gawaine; and when the noble Sir Launcelot took his horse, to ride out of Carlisle, there was sobbing and weeping for pure dole of his departing. So he took his way unto Joyous Gard, that ever after he called Dolorous Gard, and thus left the court for ever.

How King Arthur and Sir Gawaine Invaded Sir Launcelot's Realm

When Sir Launcelot came again to Joyous Gard from Carlisle, he called his fellowship unto him, and asked them what they would do. Then they answered all wholly together with one voice, they would as he would do.

"My fair fellows," said he: "I must depart out of this most noble realm. And now I am to depart, it grieveth me sore, for I shall depart with no honour. A banished man departed never out of any realm with honour; and that is my heaviness, for ever I fear that after my days they will chronicle upon me that I was banished out of this land."

Then spake many noble knights: "Sir, we will never fail. Since it liked us to take a part with you in your distress and heaviness in this realm, wit ye well it shall like us as well to go in other countries with you, and there to take such part as ye do."

"My fair lords," said Sir Launcelot, "I well understand you, and, as I can, thank you. And ye shall understand, such livelihood and lands as I am born unto I shall freely share among you, and I myself will have as little as any of you, for if I have sufficient for my personal needs, I will ask none other rich array; and I trust to God to maintain you on my lands as well as ever were maintained any knights."

Then spake all the knights at once: "He have shame that will leave you. We all understand in this realm will be now no quiet, but ever strife and debate, now the fellowship of the Round Table is broken; for by the noble fellowship of the Round Table was King Arthur upborne, and by their nobleness the King and all his realm was in quiet and in rest. And a great part," they said all, "was because of your nobleness."

So, to make short tale, they packed up, and paid all that would ask them, and wholly an hundred knights departed with Sir Launcelot at once, and made avows they would never leave him for weal nor for woe. They shipped at Cardiff, and sailed unto Benwick. But to say the sooth, Sir Launcelot and his nephews were lords of all France, and of all the lands that belong unto France through Sir Launcelot's noble prowess. When he had established all these countries, he shortly called a parliament, and appointed officers for his realm. Thus Sir Launcelot rewarded his noble knights and many more, that me seemeth it were too long to rehearse.

Now leave we Sir Launcelot in his lands, and his noble knights with him, and return we again unto King Arthur and to Sir Gawaine, that made a great host ready, to the number of three-score thousand. All things were made ready for their shipping to pass over the sea, and so they shipped at Cardiff. And there King Arthur made Sir Mordred chief ruler of all England, and also he put Queen Guenever under his governance.

So King Arthur passed over the sea, and landed upon Sir Launcelot's lands, and there burned and wasted, through the vengeance of Sir Gawaine, all that they might overrun.

When this word came to Sir Launcelot, that King Arthur and Sir Gawaine were landed upon his lands, and made a full destruction and waste, then said Sir Lionel, that was ware and wise: "My Lord, Sir Launcelot, I will give you this counsel: Let us keep our strong walled towns until they have hunger and cold, and blow upon their nails, and then let us freshly set upon them, and shred them down as sheep in a field, that aliens may take ensample for ever how they set foot upon our lands."

Then said Sir Galihud unto Sir Launcelot, "Sir, here be knights come of king's blood that will not long droop; therefore give us leave, like as we be knights, to meet them in the field, and we shall slay them, that they shall curse the time that ever they came into this country."

Then spake all at once seven brethren of North Wales,—and they were seven noble knights, a man might seek in seven lands ere he might find such seven knights: "Sir Launcelot, let us ride out with Sir Galihud, for we be never wont to cower in castle, or in noble towns."

But then spake Sir Launcelot, that was master and governor of them all: "My fair lords, wit ye well I am full loath to ride out with my knights, for shedding of Christian blood; and yet my lands I understand to be full bare to sustain any host a while, for the mighty wars that whilom made King Claudas upon this country, upon my father King Ban and on mine uncle King Bors. Howbeit we will at this time keep our strong walls, and I shall send a messenger unto my lord Arthur, a treaty for to take, for better is peace than always war."

So he sent forth a damsel, and a dwarf with her, requiring King Arthur to leave his warring upon his lands. When she came to the pavilion of

King Arthur there met her a gentle knight, Sir Lucan the butler, and when he knew that she was a messenger from Sir Launcelot to the King he said: "I pray God, damsel, ye may speed well. My Lord Arthur would love Launcelot, but Sir Gawaine will not suffer him."

So Lucan led the damsel unto the King, and when she had told her tale, all the lords were full glad to advise him to be accorded with Sir Launcelot, save only Sir Gawaine, who would not turn again, now that they were past thus far upon the journey.

"Wit ye well, Sir Gawaine," said Arthur, "I will do as ye will advise me; and yet me seemeth his fair proffers were not good to be refused."

Then Sir Gawaine sent the damsel away with the answer that it was now too late for peace. And so the war went on. Sir Launcelot was never so loath to do battle, but he must needs defend himself; and when King Arthur's host besieged Benwick round about, and fast began to set up ladders, then Sir Launcelot beat them from the walls mightily.

Then upon a day it befell that Sir Gawaine came before the gates fully armed on a noble horse, with a great spear in his hand, and cried with a loud voice: "Where art thou now, thou false traitor, Launcelot? Why hidest thou thyself within holes and walls like a coward? Look out now, thou false traitor knight, and here I shall revenge upon thy body the death of my three brethren."

All this language heard Sir Launcelot, and he wist well that he must defend himself, or else be recreant. So he armed himself at all points, and mounted upon his horse, and gat a great spear in his hand, and rode out at the gate. And both the hosts were assembled, of them without and of them within, and stood in array full manly. And both parties were charged to hold them still, to see and behold the battle of these two noble knights.

Then they laid their spears in their rests, and came together as thunder. Sir Gawaine brake his spear upon Sir Launcelot in an hundred pieces unto his hand, and Sir Launcelot smote him with a greater might, so that Sir Gawaine's horse's feet raised, and the horse and he fell to the earth. Then they dressed their shields and fought with swords on foot, giving many sad strokes, so that all men on both parties had thereof passing great wonder. But Sir Launcelot withheld his courage and his wind, and kept himself wonderly covert of his might. Under his shield he traced and traversed here and there, to break Sir Gawaine's strokes and his courage, and Sir Gawaine enforced himself with all his might to destroy Sir Launcelot.

At the first ever Sir Gawaine's power increased, and right so his wind and his evil will. For a time Sir Launcelot had great pain to defend himself, but when three hours were passed, and Sir Launcelot felt that Sir Gawaine was come to his full strength, then Sir Launcelot said, "I feel that ye have done your mighty deeds; now wit you well I must do my deeds."

So he doubled his strokes, and soon smote such a buffet upon Sir Gawaine's helm that he sank down upon his side in a swoon. Anon as he did awake, he waved at Sir Launcelot as he lay, and said, "Traitor knight, wit thou well I am not yet slain; come thou near me, and perform this battle unto the uttermost."

"I will no more do than I have done," said Sir Launcelot. "When I see you on foot I will do battle upon you all the while I see you stand on your feet; but to smite a wounded man, that may not stand, God defend me from such a shame."

Then he turned and went his way towards the city, and Sir Gawaine, evermore calling him traitor knight, said, "Wit thou well, Sir Launcelot, when I am whole, I shall do battle with thee again; for I shall never leave thee till one of us be slain."

Thus this siege endured. Sir Gawaine lay sick near a month, and when he was well recovered, and ready within three days to do battle again with Sir Launcelot, right so came tidings unto Arthur from England, that made him and all his host to remove.

Of Sir Mordred's Treason

As Sir Mordred was ruler of all England he did make letters as though they came from beyond the sea, and the letters specified that King Arthur was slain in battle with Sir Launcelot. Wherefore Sir Mordred made a Parliament, and called the lords together, and there he made them to choose him king. So was he crowned at Canterbury, and held a feast there fifteen days. Afterwards he drew unto Winchester, and there he took the Queen, Guenever, and said plainly that he would wed her which was his uncle's wife.

So he made ready for the feast, and a day was prefixed when they should be wedded. Wherefore Queen Guenever was passing heavy, but she durst not discover her heart, and spake fair, and agreed to Sir Mordred's will. Then she desired of him for to go to London, to buy all manner of things that longed unto the wedding, and because of her fair speech Sir Mordred trusted her well enough, and gave her leave to go. When she came to London, she took the Tower of London, and suddenly, in all haste possible, she stuffed it with all manner of victual, and well garnished it with men, and so kept it.

Then when Sir Mordred wist and understood how he was beguiled, he was passing wroth out of measure. And, a short tale for to make, he went and laid a mighty siege about the Tower of London, and made many great assaults thereat, and threw many great engines unto them, and shot great guns. But all might not prevail Sir Mordred, because Queen Guenever, for fair speech nor for foul, would never trust to come in his hands again.

Then came the Bishop of Canterbury, the which was a noble clerk and an holy man, and thus he said to Sir Mordred: "Sir, what will ye do? Will ye first displease God, and then shame yourself and all knighthood? Leave this matter, or else I shall curse you with book and bell and candle."

"Do thou thy worst," said Sir Mordred; "wit thou well I shall defy thee."

"Sir," said the Bishop, "and wit ye well I shall not fear me to do that I ought to do. Also, when ye noise that my lord Arthur is slain, that is not so, and therefore ye will make a foul work in this land."

"Peace, thou false priest," said Sir Mordred, "for, if thou chafe me any more, I shall make strike off thy head."

So the Bishop departed, and did the curse in the haughtiest wise that might be done. Then Sir Mordred sought the Bishop of Canterbury for to slay him, and he fled, and, taking part of his goods with him, went nigh unto Glastonbury, and there lived in poverty and in holy prayers as priest-hermit in a chapel, for well he understood that mischievous war was at hand.

Then came word to Sir Mordred that King Arthur had raised the siege from Sir Launcelot, and was coming homeward with a great host, to be avenged upon Sir Mordred. Wherefore Sir Mordred made write writs to all the barony of this land, and much people drew to him, for then was the common voice among them, that with Arthur was none other life but war and strife, and with Sir Mordred was great joy and bliss. Thus was Sir Arthur depraved and evil said of, and many there were that King Arthur had made up of naught, and had given lands to, who might not then say of him a good word.

Lo all ye Englishmen, see ye not what a mischief here was, for Arthur was the most king and knight of the world, and most loved the fellowship of noble knights, and by him they were all upholden. Now might not these Englishmen hold us content with him. Lo, thus was the old custom and usage of this land, and men say, that we of this land have not yet lost nor forgotten that custom and usage. Alas, this is a great fault of all Englishmen, for there may no thing please us. And so fared the people at that time; they were better pleased with Sir Mordred than they were with King Arthur, and much people drew unto Sir Mordred, and said they would abide with him for better and for worse.

So Sir Mordred drew with a great host to Dover, for there he heard say that Sir Arthur would arrive, and so he thought to beat his own uncle from his lands. And the most part of all England held with Sir Mordred, the people were so new-fangle.

As Sir Mordred was at Dover with his host, there came King Arthur with a great navy of ships, galleys, and carracks. And there was Sir Mordred ready awaiting upon his landage, to keep his own uncle from landing in the country that he was king over. Then there was launching of great boats and small, full of noble men of arms, and there was much slaughter of gentle knights, and many a bold baron was laid full low on both sides. But

King Arthur was so courageous that there might no manner of knights prevent him from landing, and his knights fiercely followed him.

So they landed in spite of Sir Mordred and all his power, and they put him aback, so that he fled and all his people. When this battle was done, King Arthur let bury his dead, and then was the noble knight Sir Gawaine found in a great boat lying more than half dead. When Sir Arthur wist that Sir Gawaine was laid so low, he went unto him and made sorrow out of measure, for this sister's son was the man in the world that he most loved. Sir Gawaine felt that he must die, for he was smitten upon the old wound that Sir Launcelot had given him afore the city of Benwick. He now knew that he was the cause of this unhappy war, for had Sir Launcelot remained with the King, it would never have been, and now King Arthur would sore miss his brave knights of the Round Table.

Then he prayed his uncle that he might have paper, pen, and ink, and when they were brought, he with his own hand wrote thus, as the French book maketh mention: "Unto Sir Launcelot, flower of all noble knights that ever I heard of, or saw by my days, I, Sir Gawaine, King Lot's son of Orkney, sister's son unto the noble King Arthur, send thee greeting, and let thee have knowledge, that this tenth day of May, through the same wound that thou gavest me I am come to my death. And I will that all the world wit that I, Sir Gawaine, knight of the Table Round, sought my death; it came not through thy deserving, but it was mine own seeking. Wherefore I beseech thee, Sir Launcelot, to return again unto this realm, and see my tomb, and pray some prayer, more or less, for my soul. For all the love that ever was betwixt us, make no tarrying, but come over the sea in all haste, that thou mayest with thy noble knights rescue that noble king that made thee knight, that is my lord Arthur, for he is full straitly bestead with a false traitor, my half-brother, Sir Mordred. We all landed upon him and his host at Dover, and there put him to flight, and there it misfortuned me to be stricken in the same wound the which I had of thy hand, Sir Launcelot. Of a nobler man might I not be slain. This letter was written but two hours and an half afore my death, with mine own hand, and so subscribed with part of my heart's blood."

Then Sir Gawaine wept, and King Arthur wept, and then they swooned both. When they awaked both, the King made Sir Gawaine to receive the sacrament, and then Sir Gawaine prayed the King to send for Sir

Launcelot, and to cherish him above all other knights. And so at the hour of noon, Sir Gawaine yielded up the spirit, and the King let inter him in a chapel within Dover Castle.

Then was it told King Arthur that Sir Mordred had pitched a new field upon Barham Down. Upon the morn the King rode thither to him, and there was a great battle betwixt them, and much people were slain on both parties. But at the last Sir Arthur's party stood best, and Sir Mordred and his party fled to Canterbury. Upon this much people drew unto King Arthur, and he went with his host down by the seaside, westward towards Salisbury, and there was a day assigned between him and Sir Mordred when they should meet in battle upon a down beside Salisbury, not far from the sea.

In the night before the battle King Arthur dreamed a wonderful dream, and it seemed to him verily that there came Sir Gawaine unto him, and said; "God giveth me leave to come hither for to warn you that, if ye fight to-morn with Sir Mordred, as ye both have assigned, doubt ye not ye must be slain, and the most part of your people on both parties. For the great grace and goodness that Almighty Jesu hath unto you, and for pity of you and many other good men that there shall be slain, God hath sent me to you, of His special grace, to give you warning, that in no wise ye do battle to-morn, but that ye take a treaty for a month; and proffer ye largely, so as to-morn to be put in delay, for within a month shall come Sir Launcelot, with all his noble knights, and rescue you honourably, and slay Sir Mordred and all that ever will hold with him."

Then Sir Gawaine vanished, and anon the King commanded Sir Lucan and his brother, Sir Bedivere, with two bishops with them, and charged them to take a treaty for a month with Sir Mordred in any wise they might. So then they departed, and came to Sir Mordred, where he had a grim host of an hundred thousand men. There they entreated Sir Mordred long time, and at the last he was agreed to have Cornwall and Kent by King Arthur's days, and after the days of King Arthur all England.

Of Arthur's Last Great Battle in the West

Sir Lucan and Sir Bedivere were agreed with Sir Mordred that King Arthur and he should meet betwixt both their hosts, for to conclude the treaty they had made, and every each of them should bring fourteen persons. And they came with this word unto King Arthur. Then said he, "I am glad that this is done."

So Arthur made ready to go into the field, and when he would depart, he warned all his hosts that if they saw any sword drawn, they should come on fiercely, and slay that traitor Sir Mordred, for he in no wise trusted him. In like manner Sir Mordred warned his host: "If ye see any sword drawn, look that ye come on fiercely, and so slay all that ever before you stand, for in no wise will I trust for this treaty. I know well mine uncle will be avenged upon me."

So they met as their appointment was, and they were agreed and accorded thoroughly; and wine was fetched, and they drank. Right so came an adder out of a little heath bush, and it stung a knight on the foot. When the knight felt himself stung, he looked down and saw the adder; then he drew his sword to slay the adder, and thought of none other harm. But when the hosts on both parties saw the sword drawn, then they blew trumpets, and horns, and shouted grimly. And so both hosts dressed them together.

King Arthur took his horse, and said, "Alas this unhappy day," and so rode to his party; and Sir Mordred did likewise. And never was there seen a dolefuller battle in any Christian land, for there was but rushing and riding, foining, and striking, and many a grim word was there spoken either to other, and there was given many a deadly stroke. Thus they fought all the long day, and never stinted, till the noble knights were laid to the cold ground. And ever they fought still, till it was near night, and by that time were there an hundred thousand laid dead upon the down.

Then the King looked about him, and was ware, that of all his host and of all his good knights were left no more alive but two knights, that was Sir Lucan the butler, and his brother Sir Bedivere, and even they were full sore wounded.

"Jesu, mercy," said the King, "where are all my noble knights become? Alas that ever I should see this doleful day. Now I am come to mine end. But would to God that I wist where is that traitor Sir Mordred, that hath caused all this mischief."

Then was King Arthur ware where Sir Mordred leaned upon his sword among a great heap of dead men. "Now give me my spear," said Arthur unto Sir Lucan, "for yonder I have espied the traitor that all this woe hath wrought."

"Sir, let him be," said Sir Lucan. "If ye pass this evil day, ye shall be right well revenged upon him. My lord remember ye of your night's dream, and what the spirit of Sir Gawaine told you last night. God of His great goodness hath preserved you hitherto. Therefore, for God's sake, my lord, leave off with this. For blessed be God, ye have won the field, for here we be three alive, and with Sir Mordred is none. If ye leave off now, this wicked day of destiny is past."

"Tide me death, betide me life," saith the King, "now I see him yonder alone, he shall never escape mine hands, for at a better avail shall I never have him." Then he gat his spear in both his hands, and ran towards Sir Mordred, crying, "Traitor, now is thy death day come."

When Sir Mordred heard Sir Arthur, he ran unto him with his sword drawn in his hand, and then King Arthur smote him under the shield with a foin of his spear throughout the body. When Sir Mordred felt that he had his death's wound, he thrust himself, with the might that he had, up to the bur of King Arthur's spear. And right so he smote his uncle Arthur with his sword holden in both his hands, on the side of the head so that the sword pierced the helmet and the brain-pan, and therewithal Sir Mordred fell stark dead to the earth.

And the noble Arthur fell in a swoon to the earth, and there he swooned ofttimes. And Sir Lucan and Sir Bedivere ofttimes heaved him up, and so weakly they led him betwixt them both to a little chapel not far from the seaside.

Of the Passing of King Arthur

When the King was laid in the chapel he thought himself well eased. Then heard they people cry in the field, and Sir Lucan went out to wit what the noise betokened. As he went he saw and heard in the moonlight how the plunderers and robbers were come into the battlefield to pillage and rob many a full noble knight of rings and jewels; and who that were not dead all out, there they slew them for their harness and their riches.

When Sir Lucan understood this work, he came to the King as soon as he might, and told him all what he had heard and seen. "Therefore by my advice," said Sir Lucan, "it is best that we bring you to some town."

"I would it were so," said the King, "but I may not stand, my head works so. Ah, Sir Launcelot, this day have I sore missed thee. Alas, that ever I was against thee, for now have I my death, whereof Sir Gawaine me warned in my dream."

Then Sir Lucan and Sir Bedivere took up the King, and in the lifting the King swooned, and Sir Lucan, that was grievously wounded in many places, also fell in a swoon with the lift, and therewith the noble knight died. When King Arthur came to himself again, he beheld Sir Lucan dead and Sir Bedivere weeping for his brother, and he said: "This is unto me a full heavy sight to see this noble duke so die for my sake, for he would have holpen me that had more need of help than I. Yet, Sir Bedivere, weeping and mourning will not avail me; for wit thou well, if I might live myself, the death of Sir Lucan would grieve me evermore. But my time hieth fast. Therefore, Sir Bedivere, take thou Excalibur, my good sword, and go with it to yonder waterside, and when thou comest there, I charge thee throw my sword in that water, and come again, and tell me what thou there seest."

"My lord," said Bedivere, "your commandment shall be done, and I will lightly bring you word again."

So Sir Bedivere departed, and by the way he beheld that noble sword, whose pommel and haft were all of precious stones, and then he said to himself, "If I throw this rich sword in the water, thereof shall never come good, but harm and loss."

Then Sir Bedivere hid Excalibur under a tree, and as soon as he might he came again unto the King, and said he had been at the water, and had thrown the sword into the water.

"What sawest thou there?" said the King.

"Sir," he said, "I saw nothing but waves and winds."

"That is untruly said of thee," said the King; "therefore go thou lightly again, and do my command as thou art to me lief and dear; spare not, but throw it."

Then Sir Bedivere returned again, and took the sword in his hand; and then him thought it sin and shame to throw away that noble sword. And so again he hid the sword, and returned, and told the King that he had been at the water, and done his commandment.

"What sawest thou there?" said the King.

"Sir," he said, "I saw nothing but the waters lap and the waves toss."

"Ah, traitor, untrue," said King Arthur, "now hast thou betrayed me twice. Who would have thought that thou that hast been to me so lief and dear, and that art named a noble knight, wouldest betray me for the riches of the sword. But now go again lightly, for thy long tarrying putteth me in great jeopardy of my life, for I have taken cold. And unless thou do now as I bid thee, if ever I may see thee, I shall slay thee with mine own hands, for thou wouldest for my rich sword see me dead."

Then Sir Bedivere departed, and went to the sword, and lightly took it up, and went to the waterside. There he bound the girdle about the hilts, and then he threw the sword as far into the water as he might. And there came an arm and an hand above the water, and met it, and caught it, and so shook it thrice and brandished, and then vanished away the hand with the sword in the water.

So Sir Bedivere came again to the King, and told him what he saw. "Alas," said the King, "help me thence, for I fear me I have tarried over long."

Then Sir Bedivere took the King upon his back, and so went with him to that waterside. And when they were at the waterside, even fast by the bank hove a little barge, with many fair ladies in it, and among them all was a queen, and all they had black hoods, and all they wept and shrieked when they saw King Arthur.

[Illustration: The Passing of Arthur]

"Now put me into the barge," said the King; and so he did softly. And there received him three queens with great mourning, and so they set him down, and in one of their laps King Arthur laid his head, and then that queen said, "Ah, dear brother, why have ye tarried so long from me? Alas, this wound on your head hath caught over much cold."

And so then they rowed from the land, and Sir Bedivere beheld all these ladies go from him. Then he cried, "Ah, my lord Arthur, what shall become of me now ye go from me, and leave me here alone among mine enemies!"

"Comfort thyself," said the King, "and do as well as thou mayest, for in me is no trust for to trust in. For I will into the vale of Avilion, to heal me of my grievous wound. And if thou hear never more of me, pray for my soul."

Ever the queens and the ladies wept and shrieked, that it was pity to hear. And as soon as Sir Bedivere had lost the sight of the barge he wept and wailed, and so took the forest, and he went all that night; and in the morning he was ware betwixt two ancient cliffs of a chapel and an hermitage, and he was glad.

When he came into the chapel he saw a hermit praying by a tomb new graven. The hermit was the Bishop of Canterbury that Sir Mordred had banished, and Sir Bedivere asked him what man was there interred.

"Fair son," said the hermit, "I wot not verily, but this night, at midnight, here came a number of ladies, and brought hither a dead corpse, and prayed me to bury him; and here they offered an hundred tapers, and gave me an hundred besants."

Then Sir Bedivere knew that King Arthur lay buried in that chapel, and he prayed the hermit that he might abide with him still there. So there abode Sir Bedivere with the hermit, that was tofore Bishop of Canterbury, and there Sir Bedivere put on poor clothes, and served the hermit full lowly in fasting and in prayers.

Thus of Arthur I find never more written in books that be authorised, nor more of the certainty of his death heard I tell, but that he was thus led away in a ship wherein were three queens. The hermit that some time was Bishop of Canterbury bare witness that ladies brought a knight to his burial in the chapel, but the hermit knew not in certain that it was verily the body of King Arthur;—for this tale Sir Bedivere, knight of the Round Table, made to be written.

Some men still say in many parts of England that King Arthur is not dead, but tarried by the will of our Lord Jesu in another place. And men say that he shall come again, and shall win the holy cross. I will not say it shall be so, but rather I will say, here in this world he changed his life. But many men say that there is written upon his tomb these words: "*Hic jacet Arthurus Rex quondam Rex que futurus*": "*Here lies Arthur, King that was and King that shall be.*"

Of the End of this Book

When Queen Guenever understood that King Arthur was slain, and all the noble knights, Sir Mordred and all the remnant, then she stole away, and five ladies with her, and so she went to Almesbury, and there she let make herself a nun, and lived in fasting, prayers, and alms-deeds, that all manner of people marvelled how virtuously she was changed. And there she was abbess and ruler, as reason would.

When Sir Launcelot of the Lake heard in his country that Sir Mordred was crowned king, and made war against his uncle, then he made all haste with ships and galleys to go unto England. So he passed over the sea till he came to Dover. There the people told him how that King Arthur was slain, and Sir Mordred, and an hundred thousand died on a day, and how Sir Mordred gave King Arthur there the first battle at his landing, and how there was good Sir Gawaine slain. And then certain people of the town brought him unto the castle of Dover, and showed him the tomb. And he made a dole for Sir Gawaine, and all the priests and clerks that might be gotten in the country were there and sang mass of requiem.

Two nights Sir Launcelot lay on Sir Gawaine's tomb in prayers and in weeping, and then on the third day he called his kings, dukes, earls, barons, and knights, and said thus: "My fair lords, I thank you all of your coming into this country with me; but we come too late, and that shall repent me while I live, but against death may no man rebel. Since it is so, I will myself ride and seek my lady Queen Guenever, for, as I hear say, she hath great pain and much disease. Therefore ye all abide me here fifteen days, and then, if I come not again, take your ships and your fellowship, and depart into your country."

So Sir Launcelot rode forth alone on his journey into the west country. There he sought seven or eight days, and at the last came to the nunnery where was Queen Guenever. Once only he had speech with her, and then took his horse and rode away to forsake the world, as she had done.

He rode all that day and all that night in a forest, and at the last he was ware of an hermitage and a chapel betwixt two cliffs. Thither he rode, and there found Sir Bedivere with the Bishop of Canterbury, for he was come to their hermitage. And then he besought the Bishop that he might remain there as a brother. The Bishop would gladly have it so, and there he put hermit's clothes upon Sir Launcelot, and there Sir Launcelot served God day and night with prayers and fasting.

The great host abode in Dover fifteen days, as Sir Launcelot had bidden them. Then, since Sir Launcelot did not return, Sir Bors of Ganis made them take ship and return home again to Benwick. But Sir Bors himself and others of Sir Launcelot's kin took on them to ride all England across and endlong, to seek Sir Launcelot. So Sir Bors by fortune rode so long till he came to the same chapel where Sir Launcelot and Sir Bedivere were, and he prayed the Bishop that he also might remain and be of their fellowship. So there was an habit put upon him, and there he lived in prayers and fasting. And within half a year there were come seven other knights, and when they saw Sir Launcelot, they had no list to depart, but took such an habit as he had.

Thus they remained in true devotion six years, and Sir Launcelot took the habit of priesthood. And there were none of those other knights but read in books, and holp in the worship and did bodily all manner of service. And so their horses went where they would, for they took no regard of worldly riches.

Thus upon a night there came a vision to Sir Launcelot, and charged him to haste unto Almesbury, for Queen Guenever was dead, and he should fetch the corpse and bury her by her husband, the noble King Arthur. Then Sir Launcelot rose up ere day, took seven fellows with him, and on foot they went from Glastonbury to Almesbury, the which is little more than thirty miles. They came thither within two days, for they were weak and feeble to go, and found that Queen Guenever had died but half an hour before. The ladies said she had told them all, ere she passed, that Sir Launcelot had been a priest near a twelvemonth, and that he came thither as fast as he might, to take her corpse to Glastonbury for burial.

So Sir Launcelot and his seven fellows went back on foot beside the corpse of Queen Guenever from Almesbury unto Glastonbury, and they buried her with solemn devotion in the chapel at the hermitage. When she was put in the earth Sir Launcelot swooned, for he remembered the noblesse and kindness that was both with the King and with herself, and how by his fault and his pride they were both laid full low. Then Sir Launcelot sickened more and more, and within six weeks afterwards Sir Bors and his fellows found him dead in his bed. The Bishop did his mass of requiem, and he and all the nine knights went with the corpse till they came to Joyous Gard, his own castle, and there they buried him in the choir of the chapel, as he had wished, with great devotion. Thereafter the knights went all with the Bishop of Canterbury back to his hermitage.

Then Sir Constantine of Cornwall was chosen King of England, a full noble knight that honourably ruled this realm. And this King Constantine sent for the Bishop of Canterbury, for he heard say where he was, and so was he restored unto his bishopric, and left that hermitage. Sir Bedivere was there ever still hermit to his life's end, but the French book maketh mention that Sir Bors and three of the knights that were with him at the hermitage went into the Holy Land, and there did many battles upon the miscreant Turks, and there they died upon a Good Friday, for God's sake.

Here is the end of the book of King Arthur and his noble knights of the Round Table, that when they were whole together were ever an hundred and forty. And here is the end of the Death of Arthur. I pray you all gentlemen and gentlewomen that read this book of Arthur and his knights from the beginning to the ending, pray for me while I am alive that God send me good deliverance, and when I am dead, I pray you all pray for my soul; for this book was ended the ninth year of the reign of King Edward the Fourth by Sir Thomas Maleore, knight, as Jesu help him for his great might, as he is the servant of Jesu both day and night.

Thus endeth thys noble and joyous book entytled Le Morte Darthur. Notwithstanding, it treateth of the byrth, lyf and actes of the sayd Kynge Arthur, of his noble knyghtes of the Round Table, theyr mervayllous enquestes and adventures, the achyevying of the Holy Grail, and in the end the dolourous deth and departyng out of thys world of them al. Whiche book was reduced in to englysshe by Syr Thomas Malory knyght as afore is sayd, and by me enprynted and fynyshed in the abbey Westminster the last day of July, the yere of our Lord MCCCCLXXXV.

Caxton me fieri fecit.

www.ingramcontent.com/pod-product-compliance
Lightning Source LLC
Chambersburg PA
CBHW030413310726
48979CB00002B/399

* 9 7 9 8 8 8 0 9 1 2 0 9 4 *